HINSDALE PUBLIC LIBRARY

3 1279 00149 2548

D0935024

© THE BAKER & TAYLOR CO.

THE RULES OF
THE GAME

Georges Simenon

THE RULES OF
THE GAME

Translated by Howard Curtis

A Helen and Kurt Wolff Book
Harcourt Brace Jovanovich, Publishers
San Diego   New York   London

HINSDALE PUBLIC LIBRARY
HINSDALE, ILLINOIS

HBJ

Copyright © 1955 by Georges Simenon
English translation copyright © 1988 by Georges Simenon

All rights reserved. No part of this publication
may be reproduced or transmitted in any form or
by any means, electronic or mechanical, including
photocopy, recording, or any information storage
and retrieval system, without permission in
writing from the publisher.

Requests for permission to make copies of any
part of the work should be mailed to:
Permissions, Harcourt Brace Jovanovich, Publishers,
Orlando, Florida 32887.

Library of Congress Cataloging-in-Publication Data
Simenon, Georges, 1903–
The rules of the game.
Translation of: La boule noire.
"A Helen and Kurt Wolff book."
I. Title.
PQ2637.I53B6413   1988   843'.912   88-2279
ISBN 0-15-169475-3

Designed by Kaelin Chappell

Printed in the United States of America

First edition

A B C D E

THE RULES OF
THE GAME

Chapter One

The vibration of the lawn mower's small motor passed into Higgins's arm, and through his arm into his whole body, giving him the feeling that he was living to the rhythm not of his own heart but of the machine. On this street alone there were three mowers, all more or less the same, all working at the same time, with the same angry sound, and whenever one of them stalled for a moment, others could be heard elsewhere in the neighborhood.

It was eight in the evening, the beginning of April: neither winter nor summer, neither day nor night. The sky was still light, a uniform faded blue, or perhaps a twilight gray, against which the white steeple of the Catholic church stood out clearly. A doomsday sky, Higgins would have called it as a child, but he was hardly a child now; he was forty-five, with a wife and four children, and, like most men in

Williamson at this hour, he was busy mowing the lawn around his house.

Downstairs, the lights were already on. From time to time, the track of his mower brought him close to the window of the kitchen, where his wife was doing the dishes.

This was an important evening for him, a crucial eveing, no one suspected how crucial, not Nora, not even his friend Bill Carney, who would be phoning any time now.

It was still too early to get the news. Higgins did not know exactly how things worked over there, but Bill had given him a rough idea.

"The admissions committee meets on the first Tuesday of every month."

Higgins had been surprised by this, surprised and worried.

"Does that mean there are applications every month?"

"Not necessarily."

"But the committee meets anyway?"

"We meet in the bar and have a few drinks. Somebody asks: 'Any work this evening?' And the secretary says: 'Yes— an application.' "

If he had walked just a hundred yards up Prospect Street, Higgins would have had a view of part of the lake and, by the lakeside, the long, slate-roofed buildings of the country club. He had been there twice to play golf at Bill's invitation; he particularly remembered the locker room and its smell of wet shoes, and the bar, which had dark oak paneling and red and white hunting prints. He had been impressed, also, by the red-haired bartender in the immaculate white jacket, and had envied the self-assurance with which Bill had ordered his favorite whisky with a mere gesture of the hand.

Around three this afternoon, he had not been able to stop himself from phoning Bill at the drugstore.

"It's Walter."

Why had his friend seemed, for once, reluctant to speak to him, his voice lacking its usual warmth? But maybe he had imagined it. Bill Carney was more than six feet tall and weighed about two hundred and fifty pounds. His eyes were blue and his skin as clear as a baby's. By the look of him, you could guess he'd played football in college. He was the kind of jovial fellow who slapped you heartily on the back whenever he saw you, and it was hard to imagine him without a cigar in his mouth.

"Look, I'm sorry to call you at work . . ."

"That's okay. What's up?"

Surely he hadn't already forgotten?

"It's about this evening. Do you think the meeting will take place?"

"Why shouldn't it?"

"I don't know. If a certain number of committee members can't make it . . ."

"There only have to be four of us to vote."

"Will there be four?"

"There'll be five."

"You're sure?" He had been insistent. "And what time do you expect the result?"

It had been a mistake to disturb Bill at the drugstore, where he was probably in the middle of filling a prescription or talking to a customer. Yes, that must have been it. That was why he had seemed so reluctant. He had been talking to an important customer. It was the kind of thing that happened to Higgins, too.

"I really can't say. It's very informal. We don't time our meetings like radio shows. Will you be home?"

"All evening. I won't leave."

Why had he felt the need to add, in a trembling voice: "You don't think there'll be a problem?"

3

"I've already told you, it's in the bag."

Yet he was sad, for no particular reason. Perhaps it was the hour, or this unearthly light bathing everything. The town seemed empty, dead, apart from a few lighted windows and the noise of the lawn mowers.

When he saw his wife waving to him from the kitchen door, with a saucepan in her hand, he cut the motor, feeling the same physical relief he felt at the dentist's when the drilling stopped.

He was too far away, so she didn't shout, merely pointed to the second floor. That meant that Isabel, the youngest child, was not asleep yet and wanted him. He walked to the house. In the living room, Archie, nearly thirteen, was doing his homework.

"She's been asking for you for a quarter of an hour, Dad."

"Didn't your mother go up?"

"You're the one she wants."

Even after three years, the house seemed new, and Higgins was still not used to it. He climbed the stairs and found Isabel's door ajar. Isabel was lying on her back, her eyes open in the semidarkness.

"Why aren't you asleep?"

"I need another kiss."

"This is the third time."

She was only six, but there was something in her steady look that troubled him, as if he had a guilty conscience toward her.

"Will you promise to go to sleep?"

"If I can."

"You can if you try."

"I need another story."

She never "wanted"; she always "needed."

"I already told you a story."

"It wasn't long enough."

He sat down on the edge of the bed, resigned, wondering what new adventure could befall Rick the Pig. He had had the unfortunate idea of inventing Rick one evening a year ago, when Isabel was running a temperature, and since then he had had to come up with a new story every evening. He had put Rick through every possible escapade, to the point where he now often worried about it on his way home from work.

"Close your eyes."

"You start first."

She did not know that this was no ordinary evening, that the suspense was making him almost sick, and that earlier, at dinner, he had had difficulty swallowing.

And yet it was for her, for the whole family, his wife and four children, that this was important.

Nora, still washing dishes downstairs, suspected nothing either.

Last year, he had announced to her, embarrassed without knowing why: "I've applied to join the country club."

It was about the same time of day, but later in the spring, in May, he remembered, two or three days after their older daughter's birthday. They were watching TV—they had just bought a set. The three younger children were in bed, and Florence had gone out. At first he thought Nora had not heard him. She said nothing, did not even turn her head.

"Is that all the reaction you have?"

"As long as you think it's worthwhile . . ."

His face went red, as it had this afternoon when he was talking to Bill on the phone. It always humiliated him when that happened. He knew he had done nothing wrong. On the contrary, he had done all a man could do to make his family happy and give them a secure future.

5

He had made a long speech to Nora. That was another bad sign. With his customers, especially those who came to him with a complaint, he always said too much. He knew it, but could not stop himself.

First, he explained that not only the two of them, but also their children would be able to use the club's private beach in the summer, instead of having to pick their way through the crowds at the public beach. And there were boats at the disposal of the members.

"You know very well," Nora said, "that they all own their own boats. Some of them even have two or three."

"What's to stop us buying a boat, too?"

"It'll take us another thirteen years to pay off the house."

"Everyone's in the same situation."

She said nothing more. Weeks went by.

Then one evening, Bill came over to give him the bad news: one of the committee, nobody knew who, apparently out of jealousy or just plain spite, had blackballed his application. The vote had to be unanimous; a single vote against was enough to defeat the candidate. But he nevertheless had the right to reapply the following year.

He had said nothing to Nora. Did she know about it? Had Bill, or someone else, told her? He did not mention the club again, and this year he had hesitated a long time before putting in a second application.

"Do you think I have a chance, Bill?"

"Sure! Especially now that the Colonel's not on the admissions committee."

That was Whitefield, a retired colonel who owned the best property in Williamson and wanted to see the club reserved for those whose families had been in the region for several generations.

"We've made him chairman of the entertainment committee. That'll be fun!"

"Are you sure you don't mind being my sponsor again?"

"Not at all. You can count on me."

Did any of the people deciding his fate over there, across
the lake, have any idea that at this very moment he was
telling a story about a pig named Rick?

"A long one, Dad!"

Outside, a car stopped near their house, making him jump.
Was it Bill with the result?

"There, Isabel. That's the end of the story. Rick's in bed.
Now you can go to sleep."

"Good night, Dad."

This application meant so much to him. It was important
for his family's place in Williamson society, in society in gen-
eral. Florence, their oldest, had only one friend, and spent
all her time with her, which was not natural for a girl of
eighteen. If he joined the club, she would get plenty of opportunities to change her outlook. He worried about her,
though he never mentioned it to Nora. He rarely spoke to
his wife about the things that worried him. Why was that?
They were undoubtedly the closest couple in the neighborhood.

Did she, for her part, tell him everything that went on in
her head?

He suspected not—not since the time when, after three
children, and with the youngest, Archie, seven years old,
she learned she was pregnant again. She was thirty-nine then,
and neither of them had planned for a new addition to the
family.

Nora loved children. They had never practiced birth control. But was he wrong to think that she had accepted that

7

particular pregnancy more with resignation than joy, and that, perhaps unconsciously, she held it against him? She never spoke Isabel's name as she did the others', and she often said, when talking about her: "*Your* daughter."

Did Isabel sense it? Was that why she clung to her father?

And now, at the age of forty-five, Nora was pregnant yet again, and this time she was visibly embarrassed by it—not only in the presence of neighbors but also with her children, as if she had done something shameful, something indecent.

Florence had made no comment when she learned the news; she had merely looked at her father with contempt, contempt meant not just for him but for all men.

Her brother Dave, who was sixteen, had exclaimed: "Again? I hope you don't put it in my room!"

When Higgins went downstairs, Archie, standing by the open refrigerator, was about to make himself a sandwich before going to bed.

"Are you done outside?" asked Nora.

"Not quite."

"Are you working tonight?"

"Just an hour or two."

That was another thing she didn't understand and he couldn't really explain. As manager of the supermarket, he worked long hours, sometimes starting at seven in the morning, or even at six on days when there were important deliveries, and he rarely finished before seven in the evening. The employees—the check-out people, the stockmen—put in their eight hours, but not he. Even today, he had had to stay after closing time, because of a promotional sale, starting tomorrow, for a new shoe polish. A week rarely went by without a sale of some kind. A salesman would arrive a day or two before with his publicity material, and a section of the store would have to be rearranged.

8

"How about a drink?" the most recent salesman had asked, when everything was set up, and he had pointed across the street to Jimmy's Tavern, its red neon sign already lighted well before sunset.

"No, thanks. I don't drink."

"Never?" The man seemed almost offended.

"Never."

"On a diet?"

He ended up saying yes. He always did, so people wouldn't insist. But it wasn't true. He had never drunk in his life, and not only because he had belonged, for some years now, to the Methodist church. No, he simply had no desire to.

"Have a cigar, then."

Salesmen always had their pockets stuffed with cigars, which they offered as if giving a tip. It wasn't so much to bribe people as to get them in the right mood to push their products.

"I don't smoke, either."

Was it so strange that he didn't want their cigars? Or that when a salesman tried to give him a gift, sometimes even money, he politely but firmly refused? After all, he, too, was only an employee, though a trusted employee, responsible for one of the hundred or so branches of Fairfax Supermarkets. He had started at the bottom of the ladder—first as a floor sweeper, then as a delivery man—not here, but in Old Bridge, New Jersey, where he was born.

It was because he was known to be hard-working and honest that he had been made manager of one of the stores.

And the other responsibilities he assumed, of his own free will, after his day's work—they, too, were important. He was now part of the community of Williamson—not one of the leading lights, perhaps, but someone to be reckoned with all the same. The Rotary Club had appointed him assistant secretary, and he had been invited to serve on the board for the new school complex, as treasurer, and to that he devoted at least two evenings a week.

He did not seek to be president or vice-president; he simply tried to make himself useful, and people knew they could depend on him.

"Good night, Dad."

"Good night, Archie. Isn't Dave back yet?"

"Mom let him go to the movies."

"How about Florence?"

"She must be at Lucille's."

For the past year, since she'd graduated from high school, Florence had been working at the bank, and now her father had even less idea what went on in her head than before. It often seemd to him that she was no longer really part of the family. She had her meals at home and slept there, but as if it were a boardinghouse. Her mother did not appear to be bothered by this.

"I'm going to finish the lawn," he said, leaving the house.

But it was too dark now to work properly; all the lawn mowers in the neighborhood had fallen silent. He pushed his mower into the garage, at the back of which he had fixed up a workshop. This was the part of the house where he felt most at home, perhaps because it seemed less new than the rest.

That was another thing. . . . But why go over it? Nora had been against the move. She was a creature of habit, and the old house, downtown, had been comfortable. The trouble was, who had they had for neighbors? Who lived on their street, except workers from the shoe factory, most of them with foreign names?

The children played in the street, and Nora kept her eye

on them from the window. They hadn't needed a car to get from there to Main Street.

But he had made the right decision, he was sure of that. And Nora would have proof of it soon enough, in a few minutes or in an hour, when the phone finally rang or Bill Carney's car pulled up in front of the house.

Higgins had done something a little unusual today. Late in the afternoon, he had gone into the liquor store that belonged to the supermarket. It was part of the same chain and under the same overall control, but it was in an adjoining building and had its own manager.

"A bottle of champagne, Mr. Langroll." Expecting the man to raise an eyebrow, he had tried to be casual. "It's to surprise some friends—or at least one friend."

"French champagne?"

"The best you have."

It was for Bill when he arrived with the news. Even if Bill phoned instead, Higgins would invite him over. Nora, who had had champagne only two or three times in her life, would be delighted. Without telling her about it, he had left the bottle in the car and gone to get some ice cubes from the refrigerator.

"What are you doing with all that ice?"

"I'll tell you later."

Now the champagne and the ice were in a bucket under his workbench. When he had put them there, it had seemed quite amusing. Now, as time passed, he was starting to look on the dark side. Why?

Maybe he was just tired. He had been tired all winter. He had had a bout of bronchitis, but had not taken time off to nurse it. That was the kind of thing that happened to him all the time. All his life, as far back as he could remember, he had worked harder than most other people. He had never complained. He was proud of it. It gave him an inner satisfaction that he would have found impossible to explain.

His wife also had her hands full, with four children and now a house that was almost too large to take care of. She didn't complain, either, but it wasn't the same for her. She could have lived differently, if she'd wanted to. Perhaps she would have preferred to live differently. He couldn't.

When he bent over and touched the bottle, the French label came off. He would put it back when he served the champagne, so Bill would know it didn't come from California.

"Did you close the garage?"

"Not yet. I have to go back again in a little while."

She didn't ask him why. She was not the kind of woman to pester him with questions. Yet there were times when he would have preferred her to be more inquisitive. Sometimes he wondered if she had been like that at the beginning of their relationship. It was hard to say, because in his happiness at her agreeing to marry him, he had been the one who didn't ask questions.

She wasn't from Williamson, but, like him, from Old Bridge. He was transferred to Williamson less than ten years ago. His previous job, at the Old Bridge branch, was as head of the produce department, and when Nora married him, well before that, he was still a delivery man.

They had been in the same class in high school. She knew perfectly well who he was and could not have had any illusions about him. During all the years they were classmates, it had never occurred to him to ask her for a date.

Nora's family was not rich. Her father, who worked in a wholesale hardware store, had lost his wife a few years

12

earlier, had remarried, and had two children by his second wife.

Nora was one of the most popular girls in school; one of the prettiest, too, and one of the brightest. The boys competed for the chance to take her out to the movies or to dances. For a long time, she went out with several of them, without choosing between them. Then, suddenly, she picked Bert Tyler.

Remembering this, Higgins felt no jealousy. Tyler had been somewhat wild, but he was good-looking, whereas Higgins had a big expressionless face and was as clumsy then as he was now.

Higgins had admired Nora without really being in love with her. Like his friends, he was content to envy Tyler when he saw him drive past with her in his hot rod.

When Nora graduated, she left for New York. Tyler dropped out of sight.

Why had she returned to Old Bridge? And why, one day when she was shopping at the supermarket, had she practically thrown herself at Higgins?

"Still here, Walter?"

"Oh, yes."

"Happy?"

"It looks like I'll be promoted soon."

"Going steady with anyone?"

"No." He blushed.

She noticed, but continued: "Maybe you'd like to take me to the movies some evening?"

Tyler was never seen again in Old Bridge. And, since that time, Higgins had heard nothing more about him.

It was more than a year later when he and Nora got married—and she was the one who had insisted when he objected that he didn't earn enough for two.

Now there were six of them, with another on the way, and they lived in a new house in the best neighborhood in Williamson. Had he done well or not?

So why should he now, in the prime of his life, at forty-five, suddenly start worrying? Nora would be thrilled when Bill arrived, soon, to tell them the news. The main thing was to keep calm and not let ideas come into his head, ideas he would feel ashamed of later.

"The school board again?"

"Yes."

He had fixed up an office in a corner of the living room, which his sons used for their homework. He knew what Nora was thinking: It's always *you*!

Because they always left the boring work to him, the work that took the most time and trouble. But what if it wasn't boring for him? What if he was the one who asked for this work, who kept asking for more, who considered it a privilege?

"Will the building start soon?"

"As soon as we've voted on the state's contribution." It was hard to explain, and besides, she wasn't really interested. "You can turn on the TV. It won't disturb me."

"I'm not in the mood."

"Would you rather go to bed?"

"I'm waiting for Dave to come home."

The movie was over at ten. It would take Dave a few minutes to bike home, and then he, too, would rush to the refrigerator as soon as he got in the door.

It was now after nine. What was happening at the country club? Higgins knew all of them, though not as well as he knew Bill, whom he considered a friend. He wondered who, among them, had any reason to vote against him, and couldn't think of anyone.

Dr. Rodgers was their family doctor. They had called him countless times, especially for the children. He always sat down for a minute in the living room before leaving, and his wife was one of the supermarket's best customers.

Olsen, the lawyer, was more stand-offish, but that was just because he came from Boston. He was a big drinker, and at sixty-five had been married three times. One of his sons was a friend of Dave's.

As for Louis Tomasi, owner of the elegant White Horse Inn on the road to Hartford, he was a man who ought, in theory, to be on Higgins's side, since he, too, had started at the bottom, as a waiter in a bar.

Finally, there was Oscar Blair, the shoe manufacturer, who had a dignified manner and silver hair, and who was always drunk by eleven in the morning. Yet he still managed to spend a lot of his time with a divorcée and mother of five.

Bill should have phoned by now. His silence was a bad sign. Unless, as must sometimes happen, they had started drinking and telling stories, and had forgotten that he was waiting anxiously for the result.

Bill was in politics. Recently he had been elected to the state Senate in Hartford, though it didn't seem to have turned his head. Higgins often met him at the barber's and at Rotary Club lunches.

He would have seen all of them more often if not for the fact that he didn't drink and never went to cocktail parties. Was that a reason to keep him out of the country club? The club wasn't only for drinking. There was a nine-hole golf course, which was considered one of the best in the region, and had a view of the lake for most of its length. Every week there were two or three dances, including one for young people, and in the summer they organized regattas and swimming meets on the lake, and in winter there was ice-skating.

Dr. Rodgers didn't drink, either, and only went out when he had to.

"Are you expecting a call?"

"What makes you say that?"

"I don't know. Just an idea."

He almost told her the truth. If she had found out about it, she must be wondering why he was hiding his application from her. Perhaps she thought he didn't trust her. But it wasn't a question of trust. After all, he had told her the first time. Maybe it was pride, the fear of having her see him snubbed again.

Ever since they were married, and even before, when they were going steady, he had lived in fear of not being worthy of her. It seemed to him that one day she would realize the mistake she had made in marrying him and start to regret all the opportunities she had given up for his sake.

He tried to concentrate on the papers relating to the new school. Dave finally returned, which meant that it was after ten.

"Is there anything to eat?"

He was as tall as an adult, with a man's deep voice, but he still looked and behaved like a child. They could hear him rummaging in the refrigerator. He called out, with his mouth full: "Is Florence back?"

"Not yet."

"What do the two of them do all evening, without boys?"

Still chewing, he kissed his father on the forehead.

"Night, Dad."

"Good night, Son."

"Night, Mom."

"Good night, Dave."

He was a good kid, not too bright at school, but always cooperative, always ready to lend a helping hand.

A little later, Nora, who had been reading a magazine, said: "Do you know what they're studying?"

Higgins gave a start. "Who?"

"Florence and Lucille."

"They're studying?"

"Yes. Florence hasn't said anything, but I found a book in her room. The reason they stay out so late at night is that they're studying astronomy."

He looked at Nora like a man returning from a long journey and repeated, as if he had no idea what the word meant: "Astronomy?"

His voice was so solemn, his surprise so genuine, that Nora laughed for the first time that evening, probably for the first time in several days.

"I guess they lie on the grass and look at the sky."

The phone rang. For a moment, Higgins did not dare move. He picked up the receiver, finally, with an almost superstitious fear.

"Is that you, Walter?"

Bill's voice was thick, as if he had been drinking. Other voices could be heard in the background.

"Yes, it's me. Well?"

"Well, I'm sorry. I'm even considering resigning. Apparently there's still some bastard here who . . ."

Higgins stood perfectly motionless, the receiver in his hand, waiting for the rest. But someone at the other end must have come up to Bill and tried to take the phone from him, because there was some commotion and then, abruptly, a dial tone.

Nora, who was not looking at her husband, asked in her everyday voice: "Who is it?"

Getting no reply, she looked up. Her husband still had the receiver in his hand. His features were frozen like a dead man's, and his eyes were so empty that, remembering they had just been speaking about Florence, Nora was suddenly afraid.

"Bad news?"

He swallowed, and it made a curious sound in his throat. He moved his head from left to right, and from right to left, and finally hung up.

"It's nothing," he managed to utter.

He did not look at her or turn to her once for the rest of the evening. He concentrated on his papers, occasionally turning a page to add a figure to the bottom of a column.

Florence got back at eleven, and at eleven-thirty the last light went out in the house.

Chapter Two

When the sun rose, his eyes were wide open, as if he had not closed them all night, and his face was as expressionless as it had been the previous evening, when the blow fell. Nora's warm sleeping body lay by his side. When she was pregnant, she slept on her back, and her breathing was deeper than usual, with every now and then a sudden tremor followed by a pause, during which her nostrils contracted.

That had worried Higgins when Nora was pregnant the first time, especially during the final weeks; whenever her breathing had stopped, he had held his own breath and listened, sure that she was about to die, there by his side.

He lay in bed a while longer, staring at a print on the wall—a picture of birds—which they had bought at the same time as the bedroom suite. But he did not really see it. He ached all over, as if suddenly feeling the weight of all the fatigue that had accumulated, unknown to him, over the years.

In the next room, Isabel was beginning to stir. Every morning, or almost, she half woke at sunrise, turned over in bed and moaned, then went back to sleep.

At last, cautiously, slowly, he put first one leg out, then the other, stood, and tiptoed to the bathroom. As he passed the mirror, he had a brief glimpse of an open eye below his wife's brown hair, but pretended not to notice, just as Nora said nothing and pretended to be asleep.

He often got up very early, before the rest of the family. Downstairs, he would open the kitchen door to let in the cool morning air, and then, with exactly the same movements every day, he would make himself a substantial breakfast.

This was his favorite part of the day. He never admitted it, in case the family thought he preferred to be alone and was happiest without them. It wasn't true. His feeling of well-being came from the fact that he was fresh and alert, with a new day still ahead of him.

Through the open window and door, he would see gray squirrels chasing each other across the lawn and up and down the tree trunks, blackbirds hopping, sometimes a rabbit watching him with wide eyes but not a hint of fear.

This morning, none of these little everyday things gave him the pleasure they usually did, not even the smell of coffee and of bacon sizzling in the pan. If anyone had asked him what he was thinking about, he would have replied that he wasn't thinking—which wasn't far from the truth. He had done too much thinking during the night. He had considered things from every possible point of view. People who drank too much probably felt the same emptiness when they woke up, and the same sense of shame.

He was not ashamed of anything in particular. He was simply ashamed, as if he had found himself stark naked in the middle of the supermarket, among his employees and outraged customers. That was, in fact, a dream he had often had.

The community had rejected him. Maybe that wasn't strictly true. The country club was not the whole community. But he knew what he meant.

They had let him advance, had even encouraged him, and then, at a certain point, told him firmly to advance no farther.

I'll kill them!

That was stupid. He didn't really think that. He had no intention of killing anyone. Yet, when he had got into bed last night, those were the first words that had come into his mind—as clearly as if he had uttered them out loud.

"I'll kill them."

And he had clenched his fists and his teeth, while next to him Nora slept.

Did she know? But she had said nothing. If she did know and still said nothing, that meant she, too, considered that he had been humiliated.

How many others knew? They would say nothing either, but would see him on the street and think: They put *him* in his place!

That was it, really. Or even worse than that. They were telling him he wasn't worthy of belonging to the community—to part of the community, at least! He could attend Rotary lunches, he could go home after a full day's work and busy himself with school-board work, he could march in uniform with the American Legion on the Fourth of July, but he had no right to play golf at the country club, even though one of the town's barbers had been admitted.

No reason was given. It was none of his business. Some-one who didn't have to stand up and be counted, someone whose identity he would probably never know, had black-balled him, and that was it. Too bad if he spent the rest of his life wondering why!

Above his head he heard Nora's muffled footsteps, then the sound of running water, and finally a rustling on the stairs. The door opened noiselessly, and he caught a whiff of bed.

For want of anything better, Nora said: "You're up!"

Normally, when he had to get to the store early, he told her the night before, and she drove Isabel to kindergarten. The other days, he dropped Isabel off on the way to work. The two boys caught the school bus at the corner of Maple Street. Florence, who was always the last to get up and who ate hardly any breakfast, to save time, rode to work on her bicycle.

Just as she did every day, Nora began to set the table for the children. She was wearing a pale-blue dressing gown and had no powder or makeup on.

"It looks like it's going to be a fine day."

The sun was particularly bright, and there were little mother-of-pearl clouds floating in the sky. The smell of the grass he had mowed yesterday drifted into the kitchen and mingled with the smells of the house.

"Is there a promotion this week?"

"Yes. A new shoe polish."

"Is it good?"

"Seems like it."

"I'll stop by the store about ten. Get them to save me a joint of beef."

He could have burst out laughing, and told her that it was all meaningless, that for twenty years they had lived an imaginary life. The house seemed unreal, as did the world, and the woman talking to him, his wife, with whom he had had four children, not counting the one she was carrying in her belly.

Somewhere along the line, he had been cheated. This was one of the ideas that had come to him during the night, along with so many others. When he had time, he would go back to them and think them through carefully. They couldn't all be wrong.

Did this happen to others, to sane, healthy people, the ones who were called well adjusted? Did they, too, suddenly look around them, barely recognize their houses, and think: What am I doing here?

Did husbands look at their wives after twenty years of marriage as if they were meeting them on the street for the first time?

Even the children! He could hear the boys moving around upstairs, but had no desire to see them and hurried to leave before they came down.

In the garage, he had a shock; there was the bucket, the bottle of champagne, and the label floating in the melted ice. He should have laughed, but he couldn't. Even this ludicrous bottle was no laughing matter. He would have to get rid of it somewhere, making sure that nobody saw him, as if he were committing a crime. The area around the house, the whole neighborhood, was too well groomed; it wasn't easy to find a place to throw garbage.

He placed the bottle on the car seat next to him, and instead of heading down toward Main Street made a detour, which took him close to the lake. Not to the side where the country club was situated—there was no entry there—but to the other side, to the public beach, where visitors could hire fishing boats.

The water was probably still cold. The lakeshore was a pale, thin fringe of sand and pebbles, which recalled the edge of the sea. Here and there, a trout broke the surface, causing circles to form, spread, and disappear.

He looked around to make sure nobody was watching. The only windows from which he could be seen were those of a house that belonged to a frail old woman who never left her bed.

He threw the bottle as far out as he could, muttering between his teeth: "The bastards!"

It was not like him to use that word. It had come to him during the night, with all the other things. He must have done more thinking last night than in his whole life. And yet he had slept. Several times, as he lay with clenched teeth, his thoughts and the images they evoked blurred, and he felt himself sinking into sleep, and woke a little while later with the vague memory that a disaster had befallen him.

The word seemed too strong, but it was quite accurate. What had happened in those few moments last evening, under the uncomprehending eyes of his wife, was nothing less than the collapse of everything he had doggedly built up since he had reached maturity. It was the collapse of his very self, of the Walter J. Higgins everyone knew, the Walter J. Higgins he had always known. That Higgins no longer existed, and would never exist again.

They had deceived him, betrayed him. Somewhere in Williamson, there was at least one person who must be chuckling contentedly at the thought of the clever trick he had played on Higgins.

I'll kill them!

That thought had come to him in the night, when his mind was hazy with sleep, and yet the thought had been clear, so clear that it was like a hallucination. He had worked out a

24

whole plan of revenge, but couldn't have said for sure that it wasn't all a dream.

To kill them all! That had been the point of departure, and from there his mind had taken off. He was in a unique position, he realized, to do it. He could kill, if he wanted, everyone in Williamson, or almost everyone, by poisoning a common item of food. The bread? The bacon? It would have to be thought out carefully. He would need time to get it right. But it was certainly possible, especially since, sometimes, when he dropped in on Bill Carney at the drugstore, Bill left him alone for a short while in the storeroom where the poisons were kept.

He wouldn't do it. He hadn't seriously considered it. What good would it have done him?

But in his dream, or half-dream, he had found a reason to do it, one that almost made sense: it would give him the opportunity to defend himself before the world. Not so much to defend himself, as to explain. He didn't picture very clearly the tribunal he would address, but that didn't matter. It was simply the world, society, the community.

"I've spent my life working for the community, and the community has turned around and rejected me. Now I'm a man people point at on the street, and my family has to share my undeserved shame."

It was absurd. Now, as he drove along a road damp with dew, the mist rising from the ground in the morning sun, he felt embarrassed. But wasn't it sometimes at night that you came closest to the truth?

Nobody would point at him on the street. His wife and children would doubtless never learn of his humiliation. Still, he had been insulted, the victim of an injustice, he whose whole life had been based on belief in justice and trust in the community.

If he could find the one who'd wronged him—not to kill the person, just to learn who, and why . . .

That was another thing he had thought about during the night. He had considered all the members of the committee, not just once, but ten, twenty times, and each time had seen them in a different, strange light.

Yesterday, right up until the moment the telephone rang, he had thought of them as worthy citizens, had never doubted their merits or their rights, let alone their integrity.

Had he deliberately been blind because he wanted to become one of them?

When you got down to it, what was Oscar Blair, Williamson's richest and best-known citizen, but a dirty old hypocrite? People would condemn anyone else in town who led a double life like his. Blair himself, no doubt, would fire any of his employees who had a child by a woman who wasn't his wife.

Blair's mistress, Mrs. Alston, lived on Nob Hill. Her last two children had been born since her divorce from her third husband. Blair spent most of his evenings with her, and the maid told everyone that his slippers, his pajamas, and a supply of his favorite bourbon were kept in the house.

Did Mrs. Blair know? She couldn't possibly be ignorant of her husband's behavior. Nevertheless, she was president of most of the town's charities.

She was as solidly built and almost as tall as Bill Carney and had a glass eye that was a little paler than her good eye. For her visits on behalf of charity she drove a little gray car that was known to everyone in town.

She called not only on the rich, but also on those who worked hard for their living and found it difficult to make ends meet at the end of every month. With her blotchy complexion and her raucous voice, she extracted a contribution from everyone, whether for the fight against cancer or TB or for the rehabilitation of juvenile delinquents.

And yet the Blairs could have given the whole amount themselves, without making any changes in their way of life.

He didn't like thinking like this, seeing people in this light. He had always respected Mrs. Blair. Now, he felt as though he were sneering. Whenever anyone talked like this in his presence, he would feel embarrassed, as if that person were making an obscene gesture.

Now, he couldn't help himself. He hated Blair, and was starting to detest Mrs. Blair, who never hesitated to return a large basket of peaches if she found one rotten one at the bottom.

Had he closed his eyes to all this until now just for the sake of peace and quiet, and to further his ambitions?

That was another thing he resented—that they were forcing him not only to look at them in a new light but to take a fresh look at himself as well.

He liked Bill. Only yesterday, he had considered him his friend. Bill's drugstore, almost facing the supermarket, was doing well. Why, then, had be bought land on the south hill just after being elected to the state Senate and—as if by chance—a few weeks before word got out about the building of a new highway?

In the course of his endless night, Higgins had asked himself so many questions that he had given up trying to answer them.

And the others—the lawyer Olsen, Dr. Rodgers, Louis Tomasi—each had had his turn. Maybe he had been unfair to them. He felt calmer now; a new day was beginning, a day like any other, with a fixed schedule of things to do for every hour. Main Street was coming to life. The newsdealer, who was always the first to open, was standing on his doorstep, smoking a pipe. He waved hello to Higgins. He probably didn't know, since he wasn't in the club. A recent immigrant, the man still had a strong Austrian accent and spoke German with his wife.

Wouldn't what had happened to Higgins happen to him, too, eventually?

He parked his car behind the supermarket, in order to leave the whole of the parking lot for his customers. As he got out, he caught sight of his daughter bicycling to the bank. She was looking straight in front of her and did not see him. He found it strange to see his own child passing without having any idea what she was thinking, not even what she thought of him.

Why had Florence gotten it into her head to study astronomy? Why, instead of dating boys and going to dances, did she spend her evenings with just one girl friend? Did that mean she wasn't happy?

The drugstore was not open yet, and Bill, who had entered the back way, was alone. As he unlocked the front door, Higgins, on an impulse, crossed the street to speak with him. The staff had not arrived yet. The smell in the store was stronger than it was the rest of the day.

It was perfectly obvious that Bill was embarrassed and did not know how to act. It was equally obvious that he had drunk too much last night: his eyes were red and his eyelids puffy, and in his mouth he held an unlighted cigar, which he was chewing with an expression of distaste.

"Hello, Walter!" he called out, heading for the counter as if he had something important to do.

"Hello, Bill."

Bill turned his back on him to arrange some bars of pink soap.

"Disappointed?" He said it as if it were a matter of a little everyday disappointment.

"Sorry I broke the news to you so bluntly. We had a lot to drink last night. It took forever to get the meeting started. It's always like that. The minute they're settled in their armchairs in the bar, there's no way of getting them out of there."

He was talking for the sake of talking, afraid of what Higgins might say.

"When you come down to it, most of the members go there only to drink in peace, without their employees seeing them. The evenings women aren't admitted, in particular, they can hardly find their cars when they leave."

"Who voted against me?"

"I have no idea. It's a secret ballot. Maybe it's all my fault. Maybe, the way the evening was going, I should have postponed the voting to another date. I reminded them we had to decide on an application. Olsen asked who. He seemed annoyed. He was quite red in the face by then and didn't want to get out of his chair. 'Walter Higgins,' I said. And someone said, 'Again!' "

"Who did?"

"I don't remember. And even if I did, I wouldn't have the right to tell you, because at that point we were in session, and the sessions are secret. I finally got them into the committee room, and they took their drinks with them. You see how it was! When I realized you'd been blackballed, I was furious. You must have guessed that from my phone call, which they didn't let me finish. They literally grabbed the receiver out of my hand."

He was now buttoning up his long lab coat. Its whiteness brought out the fatigue on his face even more.

"I'll try and fix it at the next meeting."

"No!"

Bill finally got up the courage to look Higgins in the face, and was surprised, and a little frightened, by his expression.

"Don't tell me you're really upset about it! If you only knew the number of people who've been turned down! Not just by one vote, but sometimes by three or four, with only the sponsor voting in favor."

"Who, for example?"

Higgins knew he looked pale and tense, but he couldn't help it. His voice, too, was not the same as usual; it sounded hard.

"That's another thing that's meant to be a secret, but, between ourselves, Moselli, the barber, applied five times, and it was only because they were tired of it, or because they took pity on him, that they admitted him in the end. Maybe also because of his wife, who was ill then and trying her damnedest to get into the best society."

"Who knows?"

"What do you mean?"

"About me. Who knows I was turned down?"

"The committee, of course."

"Who else?"

"Why . . . nobody."

"Wasn't the bartender there?"

"Justin? Sure, he was in and out as usual, but he's not the kind who'd talk. If he started telling everything he knew, I can think of a few people who wouldn't dare show their faces on the street."

"You yourself told me about Moselli."

"So?"

"Why wouldn't the others do the same?"

"Listen, I have orders to attend to. You came here to bawl me out, even though I did all I could to help you. It's not

30

my fault there's someone at the club who doesn't like you, or maybe doesn't like grocers. The only thing they had against Moselli was that he was a barber. I'm ready to bring your name up again next month. It's not normal procedure, but there are precedents."

"I already told you—no."

"Look, I'm sorry. Really sorry. Apologize to your wife for me."

"She doesn't know."

"Oh?" Bill looked at him curiously. "You mean you applied without telling her?"

"Yes."

"Or your kids?"

"I didn't tell anyone."

"Why the hell are you so anxious to join the club? You don't drink, you play golf only three times a year, and you don't have a boat."

Just as he had the previous evening, Higgins stood motionless, without flinching, his body rigid, his eyes fixed on his friend. It was as if Bill had slapped him in the face. Higgins's expression became so severe that Bill regretted his tactlessness.

"I can understand your wanting to belong to it, like everyone else, but that's no reason to . . ."

Without bothering to hear him out, without saying a word, not even good-bye or thank you, Higgins turned and walked out of the drugstore. He crossed Main Street to the supermarket. His staff had arrived now, but he went in by the rear entrance.

He had to stay calm, lucid, in control of himself. There were ten people watching him, ten people who depended on him. He was responsible for them, he was their boss.

Wasn't it funny? Someone had placed his trust in him,

someone more important than all the members of the country club put together, and he had not done it lightly, but only after having put Higgins to the test for years, just as Higgins himself was now putting his subordinates to the test.

He in his turn had become a boss, but he had not yet reached the top—not like Mr. Schwartz, who had finally replaced the Fairfax heirs; not even like the regional inspector who came every week to look over the accounts. Higgins was halfway between the top and the bottom of the ladder.

Everyone said to him, as he walked through the store: "Good morning, Mr. Higgins."

Just as he himself would say, with a respectful familiarity: "Good morning, Mr. Blair . . . Good morning, Doctor . . . Good morning, Mr. Olsen."

He hated them. At this very moment, he hated them so much that his refrain of the night before rose again to his lips: I'll kill them!

Bill's attitude had disgusted him. Bill had a hangover and his breath stank. Last night, his friends must have grabbed the phone from him to stop him from telling too much. He must have had a restless night, and no doubt the first thing he had thought when he woke up was: Damn! I'll have to explain to Higgins!

Higgins was already reliving the scene that had just taken place: Bill opening his door, hoping his friend would not cross the street, then seeing him in the doorway and wondering how best to deal with the situation.

During all the time they had been together, Bill must have hoped an employee or a customer would arrive, but nobody had come to rescue him. They had been alone in the empty drugstore, and Higgins had been as tense as a man about to commit a holdup.

Had Bill been afraid of him? Had he wondered if Higgins was armed?

It seemed ludicrous, but Higgins did not smile at the thought. He remembered newspaper stories he had read, especially the one about the war veteran who went to his crippled neighbor's house and shot him point-blank because he refused to turn down his radio. When you read things like that, you told yourself such people were crazy. If Higgins had shot Bill, would that have meant he was crazy?

A huge shoe-polish can made of cardboard was hanging from the ceiling. On a table, a shoe, also ten times larger than life, was being polished by a motor-driven brush. They were for the week's promotion, and a salesgirl who could have been a movie starlet had been sent by the manufacturer to demonstrate the product to customers.

"Good morning, Mr. Higgins. My boss asked me to tell you he'll be here around eleven. He has another promotion, over in Waterbury."

Her boss was the salesman who had wanted to buy him a drink at Jimmy's and then offered him a cigar.

Higgins looked at his watch, then at the store's electric clock. Both showed eight o'clock, and he made a sign to the cashier.

"You may open, Miss Carroll."

Miss Carroll was perhaps the one person in the world who admired him. He did not really believe Nora admired him, or the children—except maybe Isabel, but that would change as she grew up.

But Miss Carroll, who lived with her mother in an apartment over the furniture store, had an almost embarrassing way of looking at him. As soon as she saw him, she seemed to catch her breath, her face suddenly took on life and color, her eyes began to sparkle, and her bosom swelled beneath her black dress.

She had been at the Williamson branch long before him. When he was appointed, she was only twenty-five, but she had looked the same then as she did now, like a plump, overgrown schoolgirl.

"The fish hasn't arrived yet, Mr. Higgins," she came to tell him as soon as she had unbolted and unlocked the front doors.

"Did you call New Haven?"

"I just had them on the line. The truck broke down and won't be here till around noon."

It did him good to think about such everyday problems, just as, earlier this morning, it had relieved him to get on with making himself breakfast.

"Do you have the pink slips?"

He had always been proud of the company he belonged to, almost as though he had created it himself.

When he was only a sweeper in the Old Bridge store, or later, when he drove a delivery truck, he had not been in a position to appreciate the finer points of the business. Now that he was a more important part of the machinery, now that he occupied what could, without exaggeration, be called a position of authority, there were days when he felt like a juggler performing a meticulously rehearsed number, flaw-lessly, in front of a spellbound audience.

He himself was the audience. He watched himself put into gear this machine he controlled, a machine that was merely part of a larger, more complicated machine.

The founder, Archibald Fairfax—whose portrait, showing an old man with white side whiskers and a high-buttoned jacket, hung in every branch—had made his fortune only because he was one of the first to offer lower prices than smaller store owners could, by means of bulk purchases. As soon as an area seemed ripe, he would open up a store with a manager who would be supplied by a central organization.

For its time, the idea must have been remarkable. It had certainly succeeded. But when Fairfax's sons and later his grandsons let the business slide, and Mr. Schwartz patiently took up the reins, the real work had begun.

It was hard to explain this work to an outsider—to show, for instance, that from the moment a customer entered a Fairfax Supermarket to the moment he, or she, left, he was not acting of his own free will, but, without knowing it, was doing what the organization wanted.

Selling was no longer a simple matter. Every day, experts studied reports sent them by men like Higgins. Hour by hour, Higgins was kept informed of the slightest fluctuations in sales, the smallest changes in customers' tastes.

Trucks crisscrossed the country, their routes often altered by radio calls, and in more than a hundred identical branches the shelves were refilled as soon as they were emptied, without the machine ever stopping or even slowing down.

Yesterday's pink, green, and blue slips were waiting on Higgins's desk. The little holes punched in them by the cash registers held a secret meaning for him.

"Hello! Get me the Hartford office, please."

He felt like himself again, now that he was once more manipulating this machine, which was like a toy, a toy as miraculous to him as an electric train set was to a child. Little by little, his face became less tense and assumed its usual air of gravity.

As he spoke on the phone, he could see the whole expanse of the store through his office window: customers coming and going, the three check-outs working without pause, the vegetables in their cellophane wrappers on the white shelves, the extensive meat section with each steak or chop individually priced, the colorful piles of canned goods, the bakery, the dairy with its fifty-two varieties of cheese.

"Hello! It's Williamson."

He did not say "Higgins." His name did not count, any more than it would in the army. It wouldn't have bothered him to have to say: "Post 233 here."

He had served in the war, but much to his dismay it was merely a continuation of his civilian life. He had genuinely wanted to fight, to be shipped out to the Philippines or North Africa or Italy, like everyone else. Instead, they made him a drill sergeant, first in a camp in Virginia, then in the south of England.

Could that be the reason someone bore a grudge against him? The idea had not occurred to him before, but as it struck him now, he blushed at the thought of how unfair that would be. He had asked four times to be transferred to a combat unit, and each time they had told him he was more useful where he was.

He had been wounded a few days before the Normandy landings, but not in combat. A V-2 had exploded on the edge of camp. He had been decorated, along with the three others who were wounded with him, one of whom died and received his medal posthumously.

Higgins was not ashamed of his war. He had given the best of himself, just as he always did at the supermarket, in his family, or in the community. He had not asked to join the American Legion or to become its secretary or to carry the flag in the Memorial Day parade last year.

Was that, too, going to be dragged through the mud? Was it the reason the vote went against him last night? If it was, then the culprit was Olsen, who had lost two of his sons in the war and resented all those who had come back alive.

"Hartford, I want to report that truck 22 was due at . . ."

Through the window in front of him, he could see Mrs. Rodgers, the doctor's wife, a slight, white-haired, fine-featured woman, daintily fingering the chickens with an ungloved hand.

A huge yellow truck suddenly pulled up outside, plunging the store into shadow.

Higgins said into the telephone: "Truck 22 is here."

Chapter Three

He was in his office, around ten, when, through the window, he saw Nora standing by the meat counter. She was not looking his way. Mostly, when she came to do her shopping, they avoided each other, so she wouldn't seem to be receiving special treatment.

Her pregnancy was far along, and her face wore the mask it had when she was pregnant with Dave, the first boy. A neighbor had said that was an almost sure sign the child would be a boy. Yet when she was pregnant with Archie, her face had been perfectly relaxed, and she had never seemed so young or so attractive. After four children, it mattered less than ever whether this one was a boy or a girl.

Nora had hardly changed in twenty years, less than most women had, or so it seemed to him. She had not grown harder, unlike so many of his customers, who, once they passed forty, began to look almost masculine.

Was she happy? Had she been happy in their life together? She had never complained. But, on the other hand, he had never seen her as lively as she was as a young girl, before her stay in New York. But wasn't that true for everyone? What bothered him, or at any rate saddened him, was that when she was at her liveliest, he had meant nothing to her; that it was only after they married that she became more sober.

He didn't want to think of that today, and yet today was the very day for asking himself questions that normally would never have occurred to him. It was *their* fault. *They* had disrupted his life. Now he was looking anxiously at the most familiar things, as if seeing them in their true light for the first time.

At noon, he was talking with the shoe-polish salesman by the front window when Florence went by, on her way home for lunch. She was sitting very upright on her bicycle, which gleamed in the sun, and her hair, almost mahogany in color, floated off the back of her neck.

Did boys think she was pretty? Did they pursue her? She was less charming, less vivacious than her mother had been at that age. She did not make heads turn, as Nora had. All four children took after their mother, but they also had his broad shoulders and, especially Florence, his big head and thick neck.

At lunchtime, other employees of the bank and the offices on Main Street made do with a sandwich and coffee at Fred's, the diner next to the movie theater. But Florence, despite the short time she had, almost always went home. So there were three for lunch, which made it their only adult meal, since the younger children had lunch at school.

When he was through with the salesman, who again insisted on offering him a drink, he walked to his car in back of the store, still thinking about Florence. He often thought about her, more than the others, not because she was the first, but because the others weren't so much of a problem.

Even when she was Isabel's age, he had never felt he understood her, and now things had got to the point where he often felt ill at ease with her, as if she were a stranger.

"Do you think she's tight-fisted?" he had asked Nora one day.

"No, I don't think so. I think it's just that when she gets an idea in her head, she'll do everything she can to see it through."

Nora seemed to know what she was talking about. Was that because women understood each other better?

When she was only twelve, Florence used to baby-sit for neighbors after school, at so much per hour—fifty cents, if he remembered right. It wasn't in order to buy ice cream or trinkets, like the other girls. She saved her money, and now she had a bank account, and nobody in the family knew how big it was.

She had been working regularly for a year now, and they let her keep what she earned, to spend on clothes or whatever else she needed. She always looked neat, but it was obvious she spent as little as possible on clothes.

When she graduated from high school, he had expected her to announce that she was planning to go to New York or Hartford to work, like several of her classmates. She seemed so separate from the rest of the family that he still wondered why she had stayed. Because she earned a good salary and could save on room and board, which would take a big chunk if she went anywhere else? Possibly.

Whenever he talked about it with Nora, she shrugged her shoulders.

"We'll see soon enough," she would say.

What Nora did not know, because he was too shy about it to confide in her, was the thing that disturbed him most about Florence—and it was something he was starting to notice in Isabel, too, though not so clearly yet.

To the boys, he was Dad, their father, just as Nora was their mother, and that seemed to be enough for them; they didn't question it. But Florence looked at him as if she were judging him, and he often felt so embarrassed, he had to turn his head away.

What *did* she think of him? Did she resent the fact that he wasn't rich, that he couldn't buy her a car—some of her friends already had them—or send her to college, or take her to the theater in New York, or give her vacations in Florida or California?

She had been to New York only four or five times, always on shopping trips, and even her visits to Hartford were few and far between.

Surely she realized that he was doing the best he could, that he had literally pulled himself up by his own bootstraps? She ought to have understood that when they were still living in New Jersey, when, in the evenings, instead of working for the Rotary Club or the school board as he did now, he had supplemented their meager income by doing bookkeeping and tax returns for small businesses and self-employed people in the area.

In those days, he was often still at work at three in the morning, even though he had to get up at six. Sometimes he didn't go to bed at all.

Not once had he felt that she was grateful, or that she had any fondness for him. Even a certain kind of pity would have pleased him at times.

She looked at him as if she was studying a colony of ants.

Did she also resent the fact that because of her brothers there wasn't enough time for her? He had no idea. He was completely in the dark. He wondered if other parents were more enlightened about dealing with their children. Some claimed to be, in all sincerity, but weren't they deceiving themselves?

The two women were at the table when he entered the kitchen, one corner of which the architect had made into a pleasant little dining area. The rule at lunchtime was that nobody waited to start eating, because neither Higgins nor Florence had regular hours.

What went on when the two women were alone like that, facing each other across the table? Did they talk more freely than when he was there? Did they occasionally talk about him?

He had that impression today, maybe because of his state of mind, so he forced himself to appear as cheerful as he could. Was he overdoing it? Florence, who had not stopped eating, threw him a disapproving look, as though he had made a fool of himself in public.

"Fine weather!" he exclaimed, glancing toward the garden, where the maple trees cast patches of vibrant shadow on the bright green of the lawn.

Nora stood up to get his lunch. Florence, who was still eating, waited until he had sat down, seemed to hesitate, and finally said: "What possessed you to apply again, after they rejected you last year?"

He felt the blood rise to his cheeks and his ears start to burn.

"Who told you that?"

"It doesn't matter. It's true, isn't it?"

"How do you know it's true?"

He was just talking in order to gain time. He had the impression that his wife was gesturing to Florence behind his back. She must know, too. Probably the whole town knew.

"Don't you understand," continued Florence, "that they'll never admit you?"

"Why not?"

"Did they admit you last year?"

"It's almost a rule to reject an applicant the first time."

"They told you that to make you feel better. Did they admit you this year?"

"Only one person voted against."

"How do you know that?"

"Bill told me."

"What's to prove he isn't lying?"

"Leave your father alone, Florence," interrupted Nora, setting a plate of cold meat and a glass of milk in front of her husband.

"It's okay," he said. "I want her to have her say."

"What do you want me to tell you?"

"How did you find out what happened?"

"Do you really want to know?"

"Absolutely."

"Ken Jarvis told me. He teased me all morning."

Jarvis was a young man of twenty-two or twenty-three. He had worked at the supermarket after high school, and then, after serving in the army, had somehow managed to get a job at the bank. Every time Higgins went there to deposit the day's receipts and it was Ken who served him, Ken would ask, with a mocking grin: "How's business, boss?"

Higgins had not treated him any harder than the rest of

43

the staff, but he had often told him he was a loafer and would never amount to anything if he didn't change his ways.

How could Ken know what happened yesterday at the club? He wasn't a member. He would never be a member; his father was one of the poorest farmers in the area.

"What exactly did he tell you?"

Looking a little pale, she plunged in.

"That they made a fool of you, and everyone knew it except you. That they expected you to apply again next year, and the year after, and so on, thinking they would finally admit you, like they did Moselli."

Instead of protesting or losing his temper, he looked at his daughter with such a pitiful expression that she had to look away.

"I'm sorry," she stammered, after a pause. "I shouldn't have."

"Shouldn't have what?"

"Told you all that. I hate Ken. He's always putting his dirty hands all over me whenever he can get me alone in a corner, just for the fun of it, because he knows I can't stand it. It was humiliating this morning, his having an excuse to make fun of me."

"It wasn't your fault."

She did not argue, but he knew from the look on her face what she was thinking: It's all the same. What you do inevitably reflects on the rest of the family.

He must have made a mistake, after all. His daughter was confirming it. There was no doubt about it: they were making a fool of him. He continued to argue, though without conviction:

"I don't see why I shouldn't belong to the club like anybody else."

Florence interrupted, almost maternally, like an adult soothing a child: "Don't think about it any more."

"Do you mind repeating what Jarvis said, word for word?"

"What's the point, Dad? I ought to have kept my mouth shut."

She stood up, put her napkin on the table, and headed for the door. As she was about to go out, she paused, came back, leaned down, and placed a furtive kiss on her father's temple.

When she had gone, there was silence for several minutes. Finally Nora said, choosing her words carefully: "You mustn't mind what she says. She isn't too well these days."

"Is she ill?"

"Not exactly. But she has her little troubles, like most young girls."

He realized, with embarrassment, that she was referring to certain female functions, and he did not insist.

"How's the promotion going?"

"Okay."

"Is the salesman happy?"

"I guess so."

In a few sentences, Florence had succeeded in changing his mood. All at once his anger, his indignation, his resentment of the committee members had left him, or, rather, had faded into the background. He was no longer thinking of them and their attitude. He was thinking of himself, and he was overcome with self-pity.

Self-pity and also irony. Deep down, he was nothing but a poor idiot who had been deceiving himself for twenty years or more.

Wasn't that the message they had given him?

How, then, could he account for the fact that an organi-

zation like the one to which he belonged, and a man like
Mr. Schwartz, who was supposed to know about such things,
had entrusted him with the position he occupied?

Wouldn't it have been better to let him sweep floors until
he reached retirement age? There were people like that, good
people who were fit only for menial jobs. He himself em-
ployed a man of sixty-eight who had never done anything
but carry boxes, and who was loved and respected by everyone. They were so used to calling him Papa that most people
had forgotten his name.

Was that the kind of work he should have done?

"Did you know?" he asked his wife, pushing away his plate,
which was still three-quarters full.

She was tempted to lie, but didn't dare.

"Yes," she admitted, reluctantly. "But I didn't know which
day the committee was due to meet."

"Who told you?"

"Bill Carney."

"When?"

"Last week, when I went to the drugstore for your pills."

"What did he say?"

"That I ought to order some new dresses for the country-
club dances, and that he wanted me to save the first dance
for him. You know what he's like. He was sure you'd told
me."

"Were you angry with me?"

"No."

"And now?"

"No."

"Do *you* think they've made a fool of me?"

Two or three seconds went by before she replied.

"Why should they make a fool of you?"

"I don't know. But someone blackballed me."

"There are jealous people everywhere."

"Florence seems hurt."

"At her age, one gets hurt easily. She can't stand Ken, and he took advantage of the situation to make fun of her. I'm sure she's forgotten all about it by now."

"Look at me, Nora."

She slowly turned toward him. Pregnancy made her features look hard.

"Yes?"

"Answer me honestly. Do you promise you'll be honest?"

"Yes."

He made an effort to hold back the tears that were rising to his eyes. He suddenly felt very moved; probably more moved, and at a deeper level, than the evening he and Nora had decided to get married.

"What do you think of me?"

He was unable to look at her, and had to turn his head away.

"You know very well, Walter. You're the best of men."

It was meaningless and it frightened him. It was a trite answer, spoken by someone who preferred to say nothing.

"But aside from that?"

"I don't know what you mean. You're good to everyone. You spend your time helping people. You're a brave man. You wear yourself out for your family."

Nora's voice broke. She was as shaken now as he was. She pushed back her chair and went around to him, her swollen belly making her movements awkward. Leaning down, she put her arm around his neck.

"I love you, Walter."

"I love you, too."

"I know. So why care what other people think?"

It wasn't what he had hoped she would say, and it did nothing to dispel his anxiety.

"What about Florence?"

"Florence is just a kid. In fact, if you want my opinion, Florence doesn't think."

He shouldn't have let himself go. Instead of comforting him, his wife had unintentionally made things worse, and he had no idea why.

Didn't what she'd just said boil down to the fact that, though others didn't accept him as one of them, it didn't matter, because he still had her?

What did that make them, in their new house on Maple Street, which had cost so much it would take another twelve years to pay for it? Pariahs? Beings different from everyone else? Fit to sell butter, meat, and canned goods, but unworthy to participate in the social life of the town?

She realized she had said the wrong thing, had succeeded only in upsetting him further, but she could think of nothing else to say. With a sigh, she went back to her place at the table and began peeling a pear.

In the course of their twenty years together, they had rarely had such a shared moment of emotion. Something similar had happened in the maternity ward just after Florence was born; then, again, one morning in the fall, full of the rustling of dead leaves, when Florence was four, and the two of them had taken her to kindergarten for the first time.

By the time the three others started kindergarten, the parents were used to it. They were still moved, but not as intensely. And when the children won prizes, they would look at each other with a mixture of joy and sadness.

Since they had moved to Williamson, each child in turn had taken part in the little ceremony that took place at the end of kindergarten, always on the same lawn, in front of the same white buildings, with the same songs and the same recitations.

Dave, the first, had been an awkward child, his belly still bulging like a baby's, his hair in a crew cut. Then it was his brother Archie's turn, and finally, a long time after, Isabel's.

Some years, he and Nora had gone to ceremonies at two schools, one after the other, then to three, as each child in turn moved from one school to the next and took his predecessor's place in the speeches and the singing.

They would see the same parents, each time a little older, and occasionally one of these would say: "That's it for me! My youngest is graduating today."

It wasn't over for them, now that Nora was pregnant again. By the time Isabel was in her last year of grade school—in the new buildings her father and his committee were busy planning—and Archie, if he continued to show the inclination, was in college, possibly at Yale, the new child would just be in kindergarten.

"Are you very sad?"

He shook his head to avoid having to speak right away.

"You look as if you'd like to cry."

He swallowed, as he had last night.

"It's nothing. It's passed."

"What were you thinking about?"

"The children."

"What about them?"

"Hard to say. Their education. The fact that they're growing up and . . ."

"And what?"

"Nothing, really."

He forced himself to smile at her reassuringly. He felt very unhappy and very tender.

"You're a good woman, Nora."

"You say that in such a funny way."

"When I married you, I never dreamed you would turn out like this."

A kind of veil fell over Nora's face, and he regretted his words, though he had meant them kindly. They were not a criticism—quite the contrary. All he had meant was that he had been so overwhelmed when she agreed to marry him that he would have taken her no matter how she was. And it was true that, seeing her in high school, nobody could have foreseen that she would turn out to be such a quiet woman, content with the dull domestic life he had given her.

"It's time I went," he sighed, and stood up.

"Are you angry with me?"

"Why should I be angry with you?"

"I get the feeling I've hurt you."

"Not at all."

It was his turn to lean down and give her a kiss near her hairline, pressing his lips to her more insistently than usual.

Very quickly, he whispered: "I'm sorry."

He did not give her time to ask him why. He wouldn't have been able to tell her, though he knew what he meant.

He was already in the drive, heading for his car when she called from the doorway: "Walter!"

"Yes?" he shouted, without going back.

"If you meet Bill or one of the others . . ."

He could guess the rest.

"I promise I'll behave myself!" he said.

Again she had failed to understand his real feelings. She was afraid he would lose his temper and make a scene, antagonize the people whose influence counted, maybe even lose his job.

That was not his intention. He would behave himself; he

would be nice to everyone, as always. When he saw Bill at the door of the drugstore, he would shout cheerfully across the street: "Hi, Bill!"

And with the correct mixture of familiarity and respect, he would say: "Hello, Mr. Blair" . . . "Hello, Doctor" . . . "Hello, Mr. Olsen."

It wasn't their fault, but his. They were right. A Higgins didn't belong in the country club. It wasn't his place, any more than it was Moselli's. After the first flush of intoxication, Moselli must have felt ill at ease. For Higgins, the country club was over and done with. He would put it out of his mind—at least for the moment.

What he was wondering now was whether Nora was unhappy, or, more precisely, whether he had failed her. She seemed to understand Florence's attitude, which suggested that she had sometimes felt the same as her daughter did. And Florence, he was now sure, felt a certain contempt for him, with perhaps a small amount of pity mixed in. The house and the family were weighing heavily on her. She probably wished she had been born somewhere else, anywhere else, and had been planning for a long time to pack her bags and go.

She hadn't gone yet only because it wasn't in her character to set off recklessly into the unknown. She knew what she wanted, and she would act only when she was sure she could reach her goal, or at least had all the winning cards in her hands.

Wasn't that something she got partly from him? He had never been adventurous either. He had stubbornly followed the same path, toward the same goal, and nothing had ever caused him to stray from it.

It was better not to think of that goal now, since it had finally eluded him. It was the country club—not as a club, of course, but as a kind of symbol, a confirmation of his success.

Their house had been one of the stages in attaining success, and for a long time it had seemed the most important, if not the final, one. It was to be not only a pleasant, comfortable house, but also a house of a particular type, in a particular part of town.

He had gone every evening after work to see how its construction was coming along, and it had seemed to him that when it was finished, his goal would be reached and all he would have to do would be to enjoy the fruits of his labor.

He had had this idea before, when they got married and he was still a delivery man, earning thirty-five dollars a week.

"When I'm head of the department," he said solemnly to Nora, "and we have two hundred dollars a month to spend . . ."

He could remember the precise moment he had uttered those words. The pupils of Old Bridge High School were giving an evening concert, and the inhabitants of the small town—not much larger than Williamson, but more industrial—were sitting in groups on the grass as night fell. The women's dresses and the men's shirts were so many bright patches in the twilight, and little insects threw themselves against the colored paper of the Chinese lanterns.

Boys wearing white shirts and pants and caps with silver braid were playing brass instruments, and a tall, thin teacher—who had died the year after—was beating time with his long arms.

Then, too, Nora was pregnant. It was the first time, so they looked on it as a mystery, something both wonderful and frightening. He had not wanted her to sit on the grass, because of the damp and the effort she would have to make to stand up again. Not without a certain pride, he had gone

52

and asked someone in the school: "Could I take a chair for my wife? She's expecting."

They were sitting under an exotic shrub with purple foliage, which gave off a sweet scent, Nora on her chair, Higgins at her feet, occasionally caressing her hand.

"When I'm head of the department and we have two hundred dollars a month to spend . . ."

Were they any happier now? She was carrying Florence then, the same Florence who, earlier, at the table, had told her father . . .

It was over. He must not think about it any more. He didn't want to think about it. Did a man like Mr. Schwartz, whom he saw once a year at the managers' meeting, ever let himself be swayed by his feelings?

They had put him in his place. Not just the committee, but his daughter, too, and then, without meaning to, his wife.

"Do what you have to do and let everything else go hang!"

Who was it who was always saying that? It was Arnold— or Mr. Arnold, as Higgins called him at the time—the manager of the Old Bridge branch, a butcher by trade, who was nostalgic for the days spent cutting up bleeding chunks of beef. Whenever things got busy, he would seize the opportunity to go and give a hand to the boys on the meat counter, his shirt sleeves rolled up and a long knife in his hand.

He, too, had died last year. Higgins had read about it in the monthly bulletin of Fairfax Supermarkets. Arnold had ended his days in a little house in Florida. His son was a lawyer in New York, and one of his daughters had married a Harvard professor.

Passing Jimmy's Tavern, where there were always truck drivers and construction workers at the bar, he suddenly regretted the fact that he didn't drink. It might be a relief, a respite, to let his thoughts go hazy until the world seemed nothing but a dream. Was that what people looked for from alcohol?

He mustn't think about it. Once he started thinking about alcohol, he would inevitably think about his mother, and then . . .

He frowned. Luckily, he had reached the store, and Miss Carroll came rushing up to him as he entered. There had been a phone call for him, from the head office in Chicago.

"Mr. Schwartz?" he asked, alarmed.

"It was a secretary. I don't know who was calling."

More worried than he ought to be, he called Chicago. His conscience was clear, but he couldn't help being anxious. Even talking with the secretary, his voice took on a new tone.

"Williamson here."

"Mr. Higgins?"

"Yes."

"Just a minute. Mr. Foster wants to speak to you."

It wasn't the big boss, but it was someone at headquarters, someone who had visited Williamson two or three times.

"Is that you, Higgins?"

"Yes, Mr. Foster. I'm sorry I wasn't here when you called."

"That's okay. You're doing a promotion today?"

"Yes."

"How's it going?"

"Fine so far. I can give you the figures."

"That won't be necessary. But I'd like you to find out the customers' reactions in the next few days."

"I'll question them as I usually do."

"No. I want a more in-depth survey. Every branch has been given the same instruction. Between ourselves—and this is in strict confidence—we're thinking of buying the company. It started off with insufficient capital, but it looks promising. Do you understand?"

"Yes, Mr. Foster."

"Naturally, I don't want you to say anything to their salesman. Don't let him see you're especially interested in the results of the promotion. If necessary, put the brakes on for a few days."

Well, well! Here was Foster talking to him almost as an equal, filling him in on the company's secret plans, and yet his own daughter . . .

He would come to terms with the situation. He had no choice. They all needed him, even Florence, who thought she was so independent.

"Will you come in here, Miss Carroll?"

"Yes, Mr. Higgins."

"Do you have the sales slips for this morning?"

"Yes, sir."

He glanced at them, quite used to adding up figures quickly.

"How's the promotion going?"

"Very well. I think that young lady's been a big hit, especially with the men."

As she was about to leave, she opened her mouth, blushed, and closed it again.

"Did you want to say something?"

"I don't know if I should."

"Please go ahead."

"Well. I found out what they did to you, and I wanted to tell you they make me feel ashamed. It's you who are too good for them. Deep down, I wonder if it isn't better the way it turned out."

"Thank you, Miss Carroll."

"You aren't angry?"

"No."

"If only you knew how much everyone here likes and respects you . . ."

He nodded in gratitude, at the same time dismissing her. Wouldn't it have been better if she, too, had kept quiet? She had uttered barely three sentences, and yet she had managed to say one word too many. Thinking she was being kind, she had said: "If only you knew how much everyone here . . ."

But what about elsewhere? What about the house on Maple Street?

Was it really only *here* that he was a man?

Chapter Four

The meeting was due to start at eight o'clock, and all around the town hall, a long building with white columns, cars were parked end to end. The sky had turned in late afternoon to a heavy, storm-laden gray. Birds could be heard singing in the still air.

About thirty rows of chairs had been arranged in the main room. At one end was a platform, with the Stars and Stripes to one side. Every seat was taken, and people were leaning against the back wall. As he drove to the meeting, Higgins had passed many latecomers.

There was a chair for him on the platform, behind the committee table. With a briefcase full of papers under his arm, he went and took his place without looking at anyone, merely nodding to his colleagues after he sat down. There was nothing to show that he was more nervous than usual.

While waiting for the chairman's gavel to announce the opening of proceedings, he let his gaze wander over the rows of faces, like a man well used to this kind of meeting.

The committee had completed its preparatory work, and all those who were interested in the new school complex had been invited to hear the reports and then vote on a resolution.

Justice of the Peace Griffith was presiding. He was an associate of Olsen in the law firm of Olsen, Griffith and Wayne. Wayne, who lived on Maple Street, a few doors from Higgins, and whose wife had just had their first baby, had joined the firm a few months earlier, replacing another young lawyer, Irwin Webb, who had left to seek his fortune in California.

It was said that Olsen had been incapable of serious work for the past twenty years and that, although he still got the lion's share of the profits, the firm continued to function only thanks to his associates. He was sitting in the front row, his face flushed as usual, with several important people, among them Herbert Jackson, representing the federal government, and the governor's chief aide, who had come specially from Hartford.

Oscar Blair rarely came to public meetings, and when he did, it was only to those concerned with charity. As expected, however, his factory manager, Norman Kellogg, who always acted as his observer and spokesman, was present. He was an elegant, fair-haired man full of self-confidence. Higgins did not like him, and dreaded his ironic smile.

At the beginning of the meeting, there was still a whitish light coming in through the high windows and mingling with the yellow electric light in the room, but by the time Griffith had finished his speech, it was getting darker outside, and a moving layer of cigarette and cigar smoke had begun to form above the heads of the audience.

Higgins had come without any preconceived ideas. When he was leaving the house, Nora had thrown him an anxious glance, to which he had replied with a smile that meant: Don't worry. I'll behave myself.

In the past three days, he had had time to get used to the vacuum that now surrounded him. It was a curious sensation, but one he found strangely pleasurable. He no longer felt he was part of a whole, as he had before. He was alone. He hadn't wanted it this way. Others had driven him to it, and he had to accept their decision. Even at home, he watched his wife and children going about their lives with a detachment that showed them to him in a new light, as if he had suddenly been able to stand back and see them clearly.

He realized that Dave, his older boy, was not just the rough but good-natured kid he had imagined him to be. Dave was in the habit of observing his father and, especially, Florence, and he occasionally made remarks to her that seemed innocuous, but nevertheless showed a certain insight.

It was rather as if, until now, Higgins had lived in a fog that blurred the outlines of things and diluted the colors. The fog had lifted and given way, not to the sun, but to a harsh light, the kind you saw sometimes in the evening, a light that brought the smallest details into sharp focus.

He had been present at a hundred meetings like this one; both political and charitable, but this was the first time he was aware of what he was tempted to call the geography of the room, since it was a projection of the geography of the town.

He had never before wondered why certain people sat in the first few rows, and others banded together in particular sections.

Yet it was as revealing as the different neighborhoods of Williamson. Even the absence of Oscar Blair was significant.

The shoe manufacturer, on whom the fate of half the population depended, was far too important to appear in person at this sort of talking match. Moreover, he had no right to antagonize one side or the other by giving an opinion on problems that in theory did not concern him.

There was someone else in the same position, a man who owned some ten farms in the neighborhood. But he divided his time between Florida and New York, where he lived in an apartment on Park Avenue, spending only a few weeks a year in Williamson. His name was Stewart Holcomb, and his family's wealth dated back to his grandparents. He, too, was represented by his manager, a Lithuanian named Krobusek.

Blair's representative, Kellogg, and Holcomb's man, Krobusek, were sitting side by side, not far from Olsen. That made a sort of nucleus, around which other important people had gathered, as well as a number of wealthy middle-aged women.

These people were not interested in the speeches or in the reports. They leaned toward each other to exchange greetings or small talk, just as they would at the theater.

The group directly behind them consisted mainly of small businessmen, plus the doctor, the assistant bank manager, the town clerk, some teachers, and finally a few people who made a good salary. In this group, some were taking notes in preparation for the discussion period.

In the half-light at the rear of the hall were tougher faces, black Italian eyes, red Irish hair, women with babies in their arms, workers who had not had time to change.

Normally Higgins would have been in the middle group. He would have taken his place there instinctively, if he had not had to sit on the platform. He noticed that Dr. Rodgers and his wife were sitting on the borders of the first two groups, as if belonging to both. As for Bill Carney, he was sitting to the left of the chairman. In his capacity as secretary of the committee, he would read the first report.

It would have been an exaggeration to claim that the meeting was fixed, since, in a little while, everyone would be free to vote. Yet it was true that the committee, having carried out the preliminary work, expected its proposals to be adopted.

The question facing them was a familiar one to Higgins. As treasurer, he knew the figures by heart, and didn't really need the papers he had brought with him. Williamson's public school had grown too small for the population. Several private houses had had to be rented, but conditions in them were unsatisfactory. It was high time to build a new, more modern school complex, one more appropriate to the growing importance of the town.

Right now, Bill was busy reading out the statistics that showed the number of children of school age ten years ago, their present number, and the numbers projected for five, ten, and fifteen years from now.

"As a result of this research," he explained, "the committee chose two projects to study. . . ."

They had been studied in depth, over a period of several months, and Higgins had borne the brunt of the work. He had been in touch both with local businessmen and with the bureau of statistics in Washington.

"The first project involves the construction of a new school complex to meet current needs. . . ."

The front rows were only half listening or not listening at all. Their minds were already made up. The group in the middle, well informed, was waiting for the discussion to start. But at the rear, people were craning their necks in order not to miss a single word or figure.

The first project was the one the committee had finally

dubbed the four-hundred-thousand-dollar project, the sum being the cost of a modern school that would suffice for some years.

"A second project was put forward and studied just as carefully: a project that would involve the construction, now, of a school that, in ten or fifteen years, would still answer to the needs of an increasing population. In a moment, our treasurer, Walter Higgins, will give you detailed figures for each project."

Project B would cost about six hundred thousand dollars. In both cases, the federal government would pay part, and the state of Connecticut part, but the lion's share of the cost would still have to be met out of local taxes.

The committee was in favor of the first project. There had not been an actual vote, but in the course of discussions the second project had come to be regarded as undesirable. Higgins would have found it difficult now to remember who had first stated this view.

In fact, things had proceeded in such a way that he had not expressed an opinion, but had simply fallen in, without realizing it, with the others' unanimous decision.

It was his turn to speak. He stood up and began to read out pages of figures, though few of his listeners were in a position to grasp them. Why did he always get the thankless tasks to perform?

Then something happened. Suddenly he was no longer reading these figures for the sake of the audience, but for himself, and he was seeing new meanings in them. As he went on, his voice fell until he was talking almost under his breath. Two or three times, people cried from the back of the hall: "Speak up!"

He was so used to working with figures that, even as he read them out, he was making new calculations—establishing, for instance, exactly how much the taxes of someone like Blair and those of a small farmer would be affected by each of the projects.

Did he have an inkling, when he sat down, of what was going to happen? Maybe. And yet he had made no decision. In theory, it seemed, he was still on *their* side.

Griffith, who was forty and whose daughter had been in school with Florence, glanced around the rows of faces.

"Does anyone want to speak?" he asked.

The members of the audience turned to one another. Nobody dared to be the first to raise his hand.

"Is everyone clear," insisted Griffith, "that we have to decide what we're going to propose to Hartford and Washington—Project A or Project B?"

A hand finally went up, in the middle rows. It was a young high-school teacher who had three children. His wife, sitting next to him, had tried to hold him back, as if afraid he would do himself no good by expressing his opinion.

"In the last ten years," he said, with a certain suppressed aggression in his voice, "according to official figures I've consulted, construction costs have doubled and, in all probability, will continue to rise at the same rate. Yet in five or eight or ten years, if we adopt Project A, the new school will again be inadequate for the population of this town."

There was applause at the rear of the hall. In the first rows, some people leaned over to whisper in their neighbors' ears. Kellogg seemed to be confiding his anxiety to Olsen, who replied with a reassuring gesture, as if to say: Let them talk! They'll vote the way we want in the end.

"Does anybody else have anything to say?"

Two or three hands had gone up. Griffith pointed to Krobusek with his gavel.

"I'm speaking on behalf of property owners," Krobusek

began, "whether they're large or small farmers, or whether they just own a house or a plot of land. Since local taxes are calculated on the basis of property, what it boils down to is that they're the ones who'll have to bear the cost of the new school. In these circumstances . . ."

He quoted figures to show, in particular, the burden that would fall on the owners of medium-sized properties, and concluded: "I don't see why we should be asked to bankrupt ourselves for the sake of children who haven't been born yet. If, tomorrow, a single industry moved out of town"—he glanced at Kellogg, as representative of the shoe industry—"then overnight even Project A would become too ambitious, given the reduction in population."

Others took the floor, including, at the rear, a man who was the worse for drink, and who stood up to say, in all seriousness: "I have eight children and, so far, three grandchildren. In ten years' time, I'll have at least twenty. My daughters take after their mother."

The audience laughed. It was difficult to get him to sit down.

Higgins had not yet made up his mind. He was frowning, but only because Bill was blowing cigar smoke in his face.

"Does anybody else have any observations to make, or anything they want clarified?"

"Just hurry up and build a school!" someone shouted. "Big or small, it'll be better than the pigsty we have now!"

Griffith was raising his gavel, ready to put the two projects to the vote, when Higgins, almost against his will, and despite the resolution he had made before coming, rose to his feet. As he did so, he looked at the audience and noticed Florence and her friend Lucille, who had just come in and were standing near the door.

Instead of stopping him, their presence spurred him on.

64

"Before we vote," he began, in a cold, hoarse voice, "I'd like to be allowed to raise a few objections."

The objections had occurred to him while he was reading his own report.

"It's quite true, as Mr. Krobusek pointed out, that it's the property owners who will bear the brunt of the building costs through their taxes."

Bill was looking him up and down, wondering what he was getting at. In the front row, Olsen sat with his chin in his hand, his watery eyes staring at him with the same detached interest with which they might have stared at a biological specimen. Florence and Lucille had not moved; they were still standing, even though someone had offered them a seat.

"The problem," he continued, his temples suddenly humming with emotion, "is that without satisfactory schools those who own factories or farms won't be able to find qualified workers—or even workers period—to keep their businesses going."

With one sentence, he had made the break, and he didn't need to look at the first few rows to know his words had cast a chill. People were putting their heads together and whispering. Dr. Rodgers, whose face he glimpsed for a moment, was frowning at him, though more, it seemed to Higgins, in surprise than in disapproval.

"Let's examine the difference, from the point of view of taxes, between Project A and Project B. . . ."

He was not getting carried away with his own importance. No, now that he had taken the step, he felt perfectly calm. He could look everyone in the face without qualms. The people at the rear seemed the most surprised. They were nudging each other and commenting quietly. Some were smiling, as if they sensed a fight brewing. The drunk with the eight children and the daughters who took after their mother was nodding and grunting: "That's great! Great!"

And his neighbors had to stop him from bursting into applause.

Was Higgins avenging himself for his turned-down application? In all conscience, he would have sworn he was not. He had no grudge against anyone in particular. Yet his speech was a declaration of war on the clan he had always worked with, the clan he had dreamed of belonging to.

How could he explain what had driven him to do it? Did Florence, there near the door, who must be more surprised than anyone, misunderstand his action, as those in the front rows did?

It was practically in an instant, without weighing pros and cons, that he had decided to make the break. He didn't know why he had yielded to the impulse, but was sure it was not out of a feeling of envy or revenge.

He had lost his faith; that was the clearest explanation. They had cast him out, and in so doing had forced him to open his eyes and see them in a new light. That report on which he had worked so long and so hard suddenly seemed a fake.

He was not being belligerent. He was simply letting them know, in front of the whole town, that he was no longer on their side.

Bill was playing with a pencil and dragging so hard on his cigar that Higgins had to wave aside the smoke. It was getting in his throat.

He did not raise his voice once, and right up to the last moment, he wondered if he would have the courage to use his strongest argument. He knew perfectly well it would give rise to sarcasm. They would see it as proof that he was acting like this only because of the disappointment he had suffered.

The reason he finally went all the way was precisely because he wanted to be honest with himself, though perhaps also, unconsciously, out of bravado and a desire for persecution.

"The difference in cost between Project A and Project B," he said, making sure each syllable was clear, "is less than the cost of the new buildings put up last year by the country club for the benefit of its sixty-three members."

This time, there were murmurs in the front rows, as if he had said something shocking, something in bad taste, or even as if he had committed an indecent act in public. But at the rear, there was a burst of applause, and there were even a few timid cheers from the middle rows.

He sat down, conscious of having done his duty. But he was worried, too, though he refused to admit it to himself. He looked for his daughter, and saw her sharing a chair with her friend, but it was impossible to guess what she was thinking. It was not just because she was too far away; it was always difficult to read Florence's face.

"Does anyone else want to speak before we vote?" asked Griffith, after a questioning glance at Olsen. He was in a hurry to get it over with, as if afraid of further complications.

Without standing, without even facing the audience, Olsen said in a loud, clear voice: "We're not here to discuss the affairs of a private club. As far as I know, we're still living in a free country."

The thing that spoiled everything was the intervention of a poultry farmer named Purchin. He was unmarried, and for several years had lived alone in a dilapidated house on the edge of town. Occasionally he could be seen drinking by himself in Jimmy's Tavern.

He demanded the floor and launched into a violent tirade, repeating Higgins's arguments and figures, and referring to

Higgins by saying: "As Comrade Higgins has demonstrated extremely well. . . ."

The audience grew restless. They let him continue for a while, but eventually people began stamping their feet rhythmically on the floor, and a voice cried out: "Go back to Moscow!"

Higgins was not listening. He sat with his head down, anxious for it all to be over. When Griffith had restored order by banging on the table with his gavel, Higgins passed him a penciled note.

"I guess it's my duty, before we vote, to read the message I've just been handed. Our treasurer, Walter Higgins, informs me that, whatever the result of the ballot, he intends to resign from the school board."

Silence. Nothing. No reaction. He wondered if the people in the room, where it was starting to get hot, had any idea of the drama that had taken place. Everyone was looking at him, and he raised his head so that they could see his face. At that moment, he almost considered himself a martyr.

"All those in favor of Project A, raise your hands."

The front rows voted in favor, as did about half the middle rows, and there were a few raised hands at the rear.

Olsen signaled to Griffith.

"Now all those against, raise your hands."

After studying the audience, Bill leaned over and whispered: "If we don't have a recount, there'll be protests tomorrow."

Indeed, it was difficult to tell which of the two groups had won the vote. The committee members discussed it among themselves in low voices. Higgins kept out of it. It was decided to distribute pieces of paper for written votes and collect them in the town hall's ballot box. The secretary went to get it. While they were waiting, people began talking to each other.

Higgins had made a mistake in not leaving immediately after tendering his resignation. There was nothing more for him to do on the platform, though he could have stayed and voted with everyone else. Now, it was more difficult to leave. Yet he stood up.

"Will you excuse me?" he asked Griffith, who watched him without protest.

Bill said nothing. Higgins did not offer his hand to anyone. He left the platform without taking his briefcase and headed for the exit. As he passed his daughter, who was still seated, he had the impression she was smiling at him.

Outside, under the colonnade, a few men were getting some air while waiting for the second vote. A warm, gentle spring rain had begun to fall.

Because of the lack of space, Higgins had parked his car quite far from the building. He was not wearing a hat, and as he walked slowly along in the darkness, rain wet his hair and rolled down his forehead.

He was not sure whether he had done the right thing. But he had acted as he thought he should, and was well aware that there might be far-reaching consequences for him.

Would the Blairs and the rest of those whose interests he had defied take their revenge by boycotting the supermarket? They were his best customers. All the people at the rear of the hall together didn't account for more than half his turnover.

There was another supermarket in Williamson. It was run by a local man and wasn't part of a chain. Downtown, there were also two or three Italian groceries, with crates of fruit and vegetables spilling out on the sidewalk.

Would Mr. Schwartz regard Higgins's action as a betrayal? If, next month, the receipts dropped by as little as twenty percent, or even ten percent, he would be sure to send an inspector to check. In an hour, he would find out what had happened.

What other job could he find at his age? Nobody in Williamson would employ him. The only people on his side were working-class or lower-middle-class people.

He smiled as he thought about it, a bitter, regretful smile. He felt lighter than he had ever felt before, as if he had suddenly escaped the laws of gravity.

Was it because there was nothing to tie him down any more?

His house, for instance; only yesterday, it had been a major source of anxiety. He and his wife were constantly worried about the payments they still had to make before it was really theirs. In addition, there were the monthly installments on the TV set, the new refrigerator, and the car.

What would happen to all that if he lost his job?

It was almost impossible to imagine. There would be nothing left! No house, no furniture, no car! He wouldn't even be able to pay the premiums on his life insurance.

He felt like laughing and crying at the same time. He did not realize right away that he had walked right past his car, which was parked opposite the laundry.

Would he have to draw on Florence's savings to meet the most urgent expenses?

Actually, it hardly mattered whether he had been right or wrong. It had to happen. The explosion had to come sooner or later. He had borne the weight of it for three days, until in the end he had almost thought he was going crazy.

Purchin had spoiled the effect by giving his words a meaning they did not have. He had not intended his speech to

70

have any political undertones. He had not been making a social protest. He had not accused or threatened anyone. He had simply presented the figures and challenged them to prove them wrong, knowing full well they couldn't.

He was retracing his steps when he saw people starting to leave the town hall. He hurried to get behind the wheel of his car and back to Maple Street. The result of the ballot did not interest him. He was sure he'd spoken to no purpose, that the clan had won. He had simply done what he had to do.

When he got home, the boys were in bed, and Nora was sewing and occasionally glancing at the TV. She seemed surprised, not at seeing him, but by the expression on his face.

"What happened?" she asked, not hiding her anxiety.

He was smiling, but it was not his normal smile, and it alarmed Nora. It was the smile of a man who had suddenly stopped taking life seriously and was going to start behaving like a child. The trouble was that he had the lined face of a man of forty-five who had worked hard all his life, and neither his lips nor his eyes were suited to a smile like that.

"We'll find out soon enough what's happened," he said in an almost playful tone. "Maybe in a month."

"What do you mean?"

"It'll depend on a lot of things. First of all, I've resigned."

"Resigned from what?"

"The school board."

"Did they criticize your report?"

"No."

"Stop walking up and down. Sit down and look at me. I don't suppose, Walter . . ."

She was studying him as if a wild idea had just come to her.

"You don't suppose what?"

"You haven't been drinking, have you?"

He burst out laughing.

"No, I haven't been drinking. I'm not going to start at my age. I simply resigned after giving them a few home truths."

"What, exactly, did you say to them?"

"I explained why the property owners were opposed to the second project, and I gave figures to prove it."

They had often discussed this together, so she knew what he was talking about.

"I thought you were in favor of the first project."

"I was."

"When did you change your mind?"

"This evening, as I was reading my report."

"Walter!"

"Yes?"

"Did you make a scene? Tell me the truth."

"I told you: I presented my ideas and backed them up with figures."

"Is that all?"

"They weren't pleased. Especially when Purchin, who's some kind of communist or anarchist, starting making an inflammatory speech."

"What did they say to you?"

"Who?"

"Bill and the others on the committee."

"Nothing. They accepted my resignation."

"They didn't ask you to resign?"

"It never even occurred to them. Though I'm sure they'd have asked me tomorrow or the day after."

"Why did you do it?"

"I have no idea."

His tone was still light-hearted, but his wife's scared expression was starting to give him a panicky feeling.

"I think it was bound to happen," he continued, more seriously. "Believe me, I know I'm right. Project A will end up costing the community more than the other one. What they don't grasp is that the part contributed by Washington and by the state comes out of everyone's taxes."

"Walter!"

"Aren't you interested?"

"Tell me honestly. Did you declare war on them?"

"They might see it that way."

"Have you thought about your job?"

The look he gave her ought to have put her on her guard.

"Yes."

"Do you realize you risk losing it?"

"Yes."

"And that if you lose it . . ."

She looked around at the walls of their house, and her gaze seemed to include the children asleep in their beds, as well as the child she was carrying inside her.

He said, "Yes," but this time with a certain viciousness, and he had to hold on to his temper to keep from exploding. When he was still a quiet man who said "amen" to everyone and dreaded the slightest sign of disapproval from his superiors, when he still believed in Maple Street and the country club, Nora had never been able to hide a certain contempt.

Who had reproached him for wanting to climb another rung of the social ladder, even though it was not so much for himself as for his family? And who had called him naïve when he was upset by his rejection? Had he received any more reassurance in his own home than he had from Bill Carney and the others?

Now he saw things as they really were. *They* had forced him to open his eyes. Had he opened them too wide to suit them? And was Nora going to be on their side, too?

He knew now that he couldn't count on her, any more than he could count on anyone else. The only person he could count on was himself.

And the truth, which he felt like shouting out loud, was that he had never really been himself. Not just because of her, of course, but partly because of her, because he had believed he wasn't worthy of her, that she was born to have another kind of life, and he therefore had to try to give it to her, no matter what the cost.

Should he tell her that to her face?

And should he tell her that when he had looked at the faces in the back rows during the meeting, he had realized he belonged with those people? It had been a joke, putting him up on the platform. They had given him titles, deputy secretary of this, treasurer of that, but nobody else had believed in any of it. They were just making fun of him.

"All you have to do is make him deputy something or other, and he'll do all the work!"

Even at the supermarket! But that was something else, which he would get back to in due time. At the moment, it wasn't ripe. He would have to think about it some more, and no doubt he would discover a few more uncomfortable truths.

Didn't Nora realize that he had been stripped bare? That he had to be left alone and given time to find his way again?

They let a man carry on for forty-five years, encouraged him, cheered him on, then they stopped him abruptly, just as he was within sight of his goal, and told him he'd taken the wrong road.

About face!

It was absurd. About face, when he had a house, a wife, four children and another on the way, as well as all those monthly installments to pay, with repossession, foreclosure facing him if he defaulted.

Maybe it *would* have been more sensible to keep quiet, to swallow his pride and keep his anger inside. Was it his fault he had exploded?

"I think you ought to go to bed. We'll talk about it again tomorrow."

Talk about what tomorrow? Why? So they could try to salvage the furniture? So she could persuade him to go and apologize?

The refrain that had obsessed him that first day came back into his mind, and he almost said it out loud. He stopped in time, afraid of scaring Nora even more.

I'll kill them!

As he stood in the middle of the room, with his arms dangling, the door opened noiselessly. It had not occurred to them to turn off the TV, so they hadn't heard steps approaching outside. It was Florence, with a scarf over her red hair and drops of water on her face and hands. She looked inquisitively at her mother and father, as if wondering if they were having a quarrel.

"Is Mom angry?" she asked him.

"I don't know."

"Have you told her?"

"Yes."

"He was great, Mom. Very calm. He almost won. He lost by only twelve votes."

He felt quite proud to have almost changed the course of events, against the wishes of the clan. At the same time, he was relieved. If he had really managed to get Project A dropped, he could never hope to escape unharmed.

This way, they might bear him a grudge, but, since nothing had been lost, their resentment might be less violent. After all, hadn't Olsen said that they were living in a free country?

75

Higgins had expressed his opinion, as was his right—his duty even, since the point of the meeting was to discuss the question.

It had been a blunder to mention the country club, but that was his affair. He had done it with the express purpose of giving them an excuse.

If they took revenge on him, wouldn't they be going against their own principles?

Nora stood up with a sigh.

"Oh, well, let's hope it'll turn out all right. In the meantime, let's get some sleep."

"You're being unfair to Dad."

"I haven't said a word against him."

"You don't seem happy."

Nora preferred not to argue with her daughter. She switched off the TV and headed for the kitchen to turn the lights out.

"Does anyone want anything to eat?"

"No, thanks," he said.

"No, thanks," echoed Florence.

She was looking at her father as if at a new man.

"Lucille also thought you were brave," she said, very quickly, without insisting.

All he knew was that he had a violent headache and a tightness in his stomach, as if he were about to vomit.

In bed, he kissed his wife on the cheek.

She kissed him back, in the darkness, and said: "You're hot."

"I feel a bit feverish," he replied, turning on his left side, as usual.

"Good night, Walter."

"Good night."

They heard the springs creaking on Florence's bed.

Chapter Five

The next day, nothing happened as he had imagined it would. He had waked up twice during the night, aching all over, his body on fire, and had thought he was really sick. That was perhaps the best answer. If, in the morning, he found he had pneumonia, or some other serious illness, he wouldn't have to face anyone for quite some time. He could stay in bed, and his wife would look after him, creating a circle of peace and quiet around him, not asking him any more questions. The only person he would see from the outside world would be Dr. Rodgers, whose presence had a calming effect.

The doctor never talked much; what little he did say, he said in a grave, earnest voice that had an almost hypnotic quality. Did he, too, have his problems? Did he sometimes have doubts about himself or about other people? Did he

ever ask himself the kind of questions that had been plagu-
ing Higgins since Tuesday night? It seemed impossible. His
face looked so serene, and a mysterious smile always hov-
ered around his lips, the smile of a man who knew all the
answers.

Bill Carney, who didn't like Dr. Rodgers and went to Dr.
Kahn instead, had said of him one day: "He's like a con-
tented mule."

Since then, Higgins had been unable to look at Dr. Rodgers without finding a resemblance between his long, gray
face and the face of a mule.

Unfortunately, when morning came, he was not ill, and
he had no reason to stay in bed. He got up early, as usual,
not to avoid his family, but because it was Saturday and he
had to get to the store early. The children always got up late
on Saturdays, especially Florence, since the bank was closed.
Each of them came down for breakfast alone, and the kitchen
didn't get cleaned up until noon.

He couldn't have said exactly what he expected, but he
had assumed, because of the scene he'd made last night, that
he'd notice some reaction among the people he saw. The
word he kept thinking of was "pariah." He had never seen a
pariah, and had only a vague idea of what it meant, but it
suggested much, and he could imagine people, most of them,
anyhow, moving out of his way as if he'd brought shame on
the community.

Wasn't that what he was after when he'd put the blame
on the country club? Everyone knew he had applied and
been rejected twice. He had attacked those whose favor he
had been seeking. He would either be treated with contempt or be made a laughingstock. Neither was disagreeable
to him. His position would be clear, and he would enjoy his

misery, the way some sick people derived a morbid pleasure from their pain.

But none of this happened. It was as if last night's incident had never taken place. The rain was still falling, gray and monotonous, like a dull toothache, and it would continue to fall all day. Cars were streaming with water, and the women coming into the supermarket had to shake out raincoats and umbrellas. Because it was Saturday, most of them had their children with them, and the store was noisy.

He deliberately stayed out of his office, except when it was essential to be there, and spent most of his time going from one department to another, like a maître d' in an expensive restaurant.

Miss Carroll had said nothing about last night and had not appeared to look at him any differently. In her normal voice, she had said: "Good morning, Mr. Higgins."

It was the same with the rest of the staff. As for the customers, they took no notice of him except to ask for information or to complain about a price.

The idea occurred to him that they were doing it on purpose, that it was a conspiracy designed to emphasize his isolation.

For instance, at one point he was standing in the doorway when Bill passed, on his way back from the barber's. He was not wearing a hat or a coat, and his body was hunched forward in the rain. Without stopping, he waved and shouted: "Hi, Walter!"

Higgins felt like calling him over and asking him what he thought of him, and what he thought about last night, but Bill was already disappearing into the drugstore.

It was almost as though everyone was deliberately behaving normally, giving him nothing to latch on to.

At ten-thirty, as he was standing by the main check-out, he asked Miss Carroll: "Has the Blairs' cook phoned yet?"

"Not yet, Mr. Higgins."

It was an important sign. On most mornings, she called about nine o'clock and read out a long list. Since she hadn't called yet, it must mean that the Blairs were ostracizing him.

At that moment, Dr. Rodgers's wife appeared. She nodded to him and headed for the meat counter, which was where she always started. As she did so, the phone rang. Miss Carroll pulled her notebook toward her. With her hand over the mouthpiece, she whispered: "The Blairs."

Later, as he was signing letters in his office, he looked through the interior window and saw Mrs. Krobusek, accompanied by her maid, buying as much as she usually did on Saturdays.

He couldn't help thinking that this indifference, this gray, neutral atmosphere surrounding him, was concerted, that it was their way of avenging themselves, by showing him that his attack had no effect on them.

A memory from childhood came back to him. Sometimes when several kids were playing together and someone younger or clumsier tried to join in, they would whisper to each other: "Leave him alone. He doesn't count."

In other words, the newcomer could run around with them, imagine he was participating in their games, but it didn't matter what he did. They ignored him. He didn't count. And not realizing it, he would try his utmost to play a role they had already declared worthless.

Wasn't that what was happening now? Weren't they telling him he didn't count?

People were coming in and greeting him, apparently cordially: "Hello, Walter!" Or: "Good morning, Mr. Higgins."

It was if he had never had anything to do with the new school, had never gotten up to speak at the meeting.

Was this a subtle way of making it clear to him that he had done something improper? Or did it mean that they had never taken him seriously?

It was not just disconcerting; it was humiliating. He had been prepared for a heroic struggle, and all he found was this vacuum.

Nobody was calling him to account. Nobody was asking him any questions—except why the price of ribs had gone up three cents since last week.

He shivered two or three times during the morning. It might have been because he had walked in the rain last night without hat or coat. And all the time, despite—or perhaps because of—this unexpected and excessive calm surrounding him, he had a premonition of impending disaster. He had no idea how it would happen, or when. It could take place at any moment. Someone could come in and suddenly start insulting him.

Despite himself, he kept an eye on the door, making a mental note of the faces. He was almost certain now that everyone who usually came in on Saturdays to do their shopping had appeared.

Meanwhile, he had not forgotten the instructions he had received from Chicago about the shoe polish. For a long time, he stood by the display, occasionally asking a housewife: "Have you used it?"

If she said, "Yes," he would ask: "Were you satisfied with the results?"

Nora came in around eleven. She said just a few words, to ask if she ought to buy some chicken. She was walking more wearily than she had recently, and the weight of her belly made her lean back as she walked. According to the doctor, she had two months to go.

By noon, nothing had happened, and it was still raining. At twelve-fifteen, he decided to go home for lunch. He didn't want Nora to think he was trying to avoid a confrontation with her. On the way, he had to stop by the garage, because his windshield wipers were not working. Purchin was there, filling his old jeep with gas. He waved at Higgins, but didn't say anything.

Higgins understood none of it any more.

The mechanic said: "It's fixed, Walter. A bad contact."

"Thanks, Jim."

He was still convinced that something was going to happen. But the blow, when it fell, came from the least expected quarter. It seemed to have nothing to do with Williamson or with the activities of Walter J. Higgins, manager of the supermarket and former treasurer of the school board.

Everyone was at the table when he got home, including Isabel and the boys. He kissed them all on the forehead before sitting down and unfolding his napkin.

"Can I go to the movies, Dad?" asked Archie, looking anxiously at his mother, who was in the habit of saying "no" even before his father had had time to open his mouth.

This time, she said nothing. Higgins noticed that she seemed to be in a bad mood.

"If your mother says it's okay."

"Let him do what he likes," she sighed.

"How about you, Dave? What are you doing this afternoon?"

"If the rain stops, I'll play baseball."

The season had not begun yet, but a lot of boys were already practicing in the town ball park. Higgins was deputy treasurer of the local team, and one evening a week he coached the Little Leaguers. Was he going to resign from those jobs, too?

"What's the matter?" he asked Nora, when she had served his lunch and sat down again.

"Nothing."

"Don't you feel well?"

She gestured to him not to continue in front of the children, and that was enough to alarm him. What had happened after he'd seen her earlier? What had upset her that she didn't want the children to hear?

The boys were in a hurry and were asking for their dessert. Isabel, as usual, was taking her time, chewing each mouthful solemnly, and looking at each of them in turn.

To Higgins, the meal seemed endless.

"Can I turn the TV on?" asked Isabel, after the boys had rushed out.

Nora, in the doorway, was calling: "Dave! Come back! Take your raincoat!"

"The rain's almost stopped, Mom."

"Come back here!"

"Can I turn the TV on, Dad?"

He said, "Yes." He wanted to be alone with Nora. Florence had gone up to her room, where she would lie on her bed, reading or writing.

Nora returned. Without finishing her dessert, she began carrying the dishes to the sink.

"What's the matter?"

"There was a phone call from Glendale."

"When?"

"Just as I got back. It's lucky I arrived in time—Archie was about to answer."

He had no idea how to put it. He didn't dare ask: "Is she dead?"

Nora simply said: "Just like the other times."

"Last night?"

"Or very early this morning. They realized at ten and phoned immediately."

"Have they notified the police?"

"Yes. But you know her."

It was so ironic, it was almost comical. Here he was, engaged in a struggle against a whole town, fighting, as it were, for what he considered his dignity as a man, and yet the blow had come, not from the people of Williamson, but from his own mother.

Now, they could expect anything. She might show up at the supermarket, or at the door of the house on Maple Street, or they might get a phone call from the police, or the sheriff, or some storekeeper.

Glendale was nearly a hundred miles away, in New York State, but she could easily have caught a bus or a train, and she was quite capable of telling a sob story and hitching a ride. It had happened once before, and he had had a hard time persuading the driver who'd brought her that he was not a cruel son. While he was trying to convince him, his mother, standing behind the man's back, was making faces, as if to say: "You asked for it!"

She always gloated in situations like that. They were the happiest moments of her life.

"Did they say if she had any money on her?"

"Do you think she hasn't? She manages to grab everything within reach."

Once, despite the fact that a close watch was kept on her, she had succeeded in unscrewing the faucet in a bathroom at Glendale and hiding it under her pillow like a treasure.

It was not a mental hospital. It was a so-called rest home, and keeping her there cost Higgins more than a quarter of his salary. He could have had her committed to a state institution. The last specialist he had spoken to had suggested it himself.

"But I can't promise you they won't release her after six months or two years. The hospitals are so overcrowded, they're forced to leave a lot of insane people at large. In any case, from a strictly legal point of view, your mother isn't insane."

At least ten times since Tuesday evening he had started thinking about her, and each time he had done his best to push the problem to the back of his mind. Even with Nora, it was a subject he preferred to avoid, and he had never confessed to her his deepest feelings about it.

Whenever anyone mentioned alcohol . . . or last night, when he looked at the faces in the darkness at the rear of the hall and told himself they were the people he belonged with . . .

How old was she now? He always had to work it out. Forty-five plus twenty-three. She was sixty-eight. She was short and slight, and looked as if a breath of wind could knock her over, and yet she had incredible energy and had never been ill in her life.

He drove out to see her two or three times a year, almost always alone. Nora had not gone with him since she became pregnant and had been advised not to travel by car. As for the children, he had not dared take any of them since he and Nora had paid a visit with Florence when she was seven.

His mother had looked her up and down and declared: "What an ugly little creature!" Once outside, Nora had noticed that the gold chain Florence wore around her neck was missing. It had never been seen again. The director of the rest home, a Dane named Andersen, said he was astounded by her tricks.

The home had only about forty patients, most of them elderly, some of them disabled. During the first few weeks she'd been there, there was a flood of complaints about personal belongings that had vanished. Higgins was summoned by phone, and he had to reason with his mother to get her to give back what she had taken.

"It's every man for himself!" was all she said. "When I've got nothing left, there'll be no one to feed me, and I've known enough hunger in my life!"

She always uttered the word "hunger" in a tragic voice, like someone who knew what it really meant. It made Higgins feel sick at heart every time.

"You know perfectly well, Mom, that I won't leave you in need."

"I don't know that at all. Every man for himself. That's the only thing life has taught me."

The people of Williamson would probably not believe it, especially now, but he had not been happy about his decision to put her in a home. His mother had not lived with him for several years before he got married. Had she ever lived with him on a regular basis? She was always disappearing, for weeks or for months on end. She didn't care where she went or what she did. She would find a job, as a waitress in a cafeteria, as a chambermaid in a hotel, as a dishwasher—it didn't matter what.

Nobody understood her peculiarities, her sudden changes of mood, until they learned that she was a secret drinker. She hid it so well that it was quite a while before anyone suspected.

The other thing people she worked for finally realized was that objects were constantly disappearing, and sometimes money as well, though only small amounts. Once, when she took two spoons and the police were called in, she answered their questions with indifference, as if what she had done was perfectly natural.

"They had too many of them. It took them a whole month to discover these two were missing."

It was this characteristic of hers the doctor had been referring to when he mentioned her legal status.

"I'm sure she steals because of an almost uncontrollable impulse. But I'm also sure she knows right from wrong. She enjoys breaking the law."

The people she stole from she mocked as mercilessly as the police.

"Where are the things you've stolen?"

"I didn't steal them. I took them."

"Where are they?"

"Find them yourself."

Often, they were never found. Somewhere or other, she always had a hiding place, or even several, where she hoarded her treasures.

The thing she found hardest to bear at Glendale was the absence of alcohol. Even so, the staff had several times found her lying drunk on her bed, though they could never discover how she had managed to get hold of the liquor. The director, discouraged, had threatened to send her back to her son.

"Why do you do it, Mom?" Higgins had asked.

She simply looked at him derisively.

"Don't you know it's wrong?"

"You'll change your tune by the time you're my age— though you'll probably be dead before then."

He was convinced she did not love him. She probably even hated him. Did she love his sister, the sister their father had taken away with him and who had never been heard of again?

It was strange to think that somewhere in the world he had a sister, who was two years older, almost certainly married, and probably a mother. All he knew about her was that her name was Patricia—Patricia Higgins. If she was married, she would have a different name, and he wouldn't recognize her if he passed her on the street. She was only three years old, and he only ten or eleven months, when she left.

Did anyone in Williamson know about his past? The night after he was blackballed, the idea had briefly occurred to him that one of the members of the admissions committee might have connections in Old Bridge and had found out about his background.

There were poor people in Williamson, too, especially around the shoe factory. Some of them were confirmed alcoholics; society had given up on them, but people were quite indulgent toward them. Then there were the O'Connors, an almost wild family who lived in a cabin on the edge of town, surrounded by garbage. Including the mother and father, there were eleven or twelve of them, plus a number of animals, more or less domesticated. Everyone in the family had abundant red hair and equally abundant good health. The two youngest, who were twins, loved to ride at top speed down the hilly streets on bicycles without tires, striking terror into the hearts of the town's mothers.

The difference was that no O'Connor had ever imagined he could belong to the country club. One of the boys, though, was more civilized, and was trying hard to make something of his life. He was sixteen and still in high school. Last summer, he had found a vacation job at the supermarket, and Higgins could not look at him without thinking of his own adolescence.

Yet the O'Connors were a real family, at least, and had never been in trouble with the police except over matters of hygiene or illegal slaughtering of animals. Higgins's origins were more dubious, and he was far from certain of them himself. He had pieced the story together bit by bit, guessing at the parts that were missing. But he was not always sure that the details, which now and then his mother took a malicious pleasure in providing him, were true.

Her name was Louisa Fuchs, and, according to her papers, she was born in Hamburg, Germany, or, more precisely, in Altona, on the other side of the river, where the shipyards were. Her father was working there when, one day when he was drunk, he fell from some scaffolding and died, leaving eight or nine orphans.

"How old were you then, Mom?"

"Fifteen. There were two older than me—Hans and Emma."

"Was your mother still alive?"

"They'd put her in a sanatorium, because her lungs were almost completely gone. Two of my brothers had TB, too. One of them died while I was still in Germany."

"Did Emma bring you up?"

She looked at him with a glint in her eye, as if he were the most naïve creature on earth.

"You're so American!"

"Didn't she take care of you?"

"She had enough to do taking care of herself. After all, she had to eat."

"What did she do?"

"What girls usually did to earn their crust of bread around the shipyards of Altona." He didn't dare ask: And what about you? He was afraid of the answer.

"At fifteen, I began working as a waitress in a café on the

waterfront. At eighteen, I managed to get on a ship with a friend of mine, a fat girl named Gertrude, who could never get enough beer, especially if someone else was paying. We landed in New York. Life wasn't as easy in those days as it is now, especially for girls who didn't know a word of English. For a year, we didn't go any farther than the area where our boat docked. We got jobs in the same hotel."

He knew she had moved around after that. She talked about Chicago, St. Louis, and New Orleans. She had one very small photograph of herself at that period: almost plump, her face surrounded by curly hair, and the same mischievous eyes she had now.

Was she already in the habit of stealing whatever she could get her hands on? Was that the reason she had moved around so much? And was it her friend Gertrude who had started her drinking?

He would like to know, and yet, at the same time, there were certain things he preferred not to face. He never learned how she ended up in Old Bridge, a small New Jersey town, more like a village, about forty-five miles from New York. She was a waitress in the town's hotel, the Devonshire Inn, when his father met her.

About his father, he knew even less. Since he was only a baby when his father left, taking Patricia with him, he didn't remember him. What was certain was that he and Louisa were legally married. She had the certificate to prove it, and kept it with her like a treasured possession.

"What did he do, Mom?"

"He was a traveling salesman."

"What did he sell?"

She looked at him with that same ironic twinkle in her eyes, but the irony was not bitter; it was cruel and malicious.

"It depended."

Then she added, deliberately: "He wasn't any better than I was."

"Did he ever go to jail?"

"Maybe before or after, but not while he was with me. True, he wasn't with me very long!"

As far as he could establish, his father had stayed at the Devonshire Inn while on business. Why he had lingered in an obscure spot like Old Bridge, hardly a promising market for a traveling salesman, was a mystery. The fact remained, however, that he had married Louisa Fuchs, and for a while they had lived in an apartment in the town. She once showed her son the building. It was a large block that looked like a barracks, and it housed some thirty families.

"He went away for two or three months at a time. Occasionally he sent a postcard or a money order. He didn't see your sister until six weeks after she was born, when he got back from California. He liked her right away. He wanted the three of us to travel around together, but I didn't want to. Then I didn't hear anything from him for a year. When he came back, I was in jail. He was the one who got me out. They've always tried to make it hard for me, and things haven't changed. Nine months later, you were born. Your head was so big, I almost died. It crippled me for the rest of my life."

It always shocked him when she came out with details like that, and he knew she did it to embarrass him.

The last psychiatrist he had consulted had said: "If it wasn't so much like a production line here, and we weren't forced to work like dogs, I'd take your mother under my wing and study her case in depth. She's one of the most remarkable characters I've ever encountered."

It was difficult to tell if she was unhappy or not. She seemed to enjoy her eccentricities. And she seemed to enjoy tormenting her son, as though she had an old score to settle with him.

"You look like him," she said one day, referring to his father. "He had a big head, too, but he had a better build and was stronger than you."

One fine day, his father had returned to Old Bridge and announced: "I'm going away and taking Patricia with me. You can keep the boy."

His mother had begged him not to take Patricia, but he had been adamant.

"The boy's too young," he had argued.

All night long, they had quarreled, and neighbors had banged on the walls to try to get some quiet. At six in the morning, he had caught the first train out, taking his little girl with him.

Nora knew the whole story—after all, she was from Old Bridge, and had known Louisa—but there were details Higgins had never told her, such as those about Germany.

During his childhood, his mother had worked as a cleaning woman, and had occasionally found a job in a bar or a hotel in the area. When she did, she would leave him in the care of a neighbor and not come back for two or three months, just as his father had done previously.

He was eight years old the first time he had to go by himself to the police station to claim her. That became a regular event in his life. The policemen greeted him cordially, and people felt sorry for him and said how good he was.

By the age of sixteen, he was used to spending most of his time alone in the one room they lived in, doing the housework and cooking his own meals.

"So you've decided to become somebody!" she would sneer

whenever she caught him with his nose buried in his school-books.

The idea made her laugh, a silent, almost threatening laugh.

"Do you really think they'll let the son of Louisa and that scum Higgins become one of them?"

She drank more and more. She was often picked up from the sidewalk and taken to the hospital. And she always managed to escape; she used every trick in the book. No longer satisfied with stealing small objects from stores, she started choosing bulky items, things that were particularly difficult to hide, even if she had absolutely no need of them. If she was caught at the exit, she tried to brazen it out.

"Prove I wasn't going to pay."

She took a real dislike to Nora right at the start, and Higgins was convinced it was to spite Nora that, a few months after their wedding, his mother announced her intention of coming to live with them. She didn't just announce it. One morning she actually showed up at their apartment with all her belongings packed in cartons tied with string.

"Well, my dear," she said, "I told myself that now that you're pregnant, you'd be glad of a helping hand around the place."

In the months that followed, he often found Nora in tears in a corner of the kitchen when he got home in the evening.

They waited patiently.

The only respite came when Louisa was charged with a more serious offense than usual and had to spend a few weeks in jail.

Finally, the district attorney summoned Higgins to his office.

"It's time you did something about her!" he said in an exasperated tone. "This farce has got to stop."

"But you know she isn't responsible for her actions."

The D.A. shot him a harsh look.

"Do you want to know what I think? That woman's no more crazy than you or me. The truth is, she's decided to get her own back for everything she's suffered in her life, and you and your wife are her main targets. I don't think she's going to give up."

"What do you advise me to do?"

"I don't care what you do. That's your affair. I just want you to get her off our backs. If you don't, next time I'll throw her in an asylum, and that'll be the end of it."

Higgins knew about asylums. They had locked her up in one once, without telling him, and he had had a lot of trouble getting her out. When he had finally been allowed to see her, in a room with fifteen or twenty other women, their hair disheveled, their clothes thrown carelessly on their bodies, she had groveled at his feet and begged him not to abandon her.

"I won't do it again," she had cried, sobbing like a little girl. "I promise I won't do it again. Don't forget I'm your mother. I carried you inside me. And now I'm only a poor old woman people point at on the street. I know you're ashamed of me. I know I cost you money. But for God's sake get me out of here. They won't even let me die in peace. I'm scared. Don't you understand? I'm scared, Walter! I'm scared!"

He had talked to several doctors, including a psychiatrist in New York, the one who said he'd like to study Louisa if he had the time. He was the one who had suggested Glendale, if Higgins could afford it.

That was eleven years ago, before they had moved away from Old Bridge. Nobody in Williamson knew Louisa. The only time she had got that far, they were living downtown, and he had taken her in hand before she had time to attract attention.

On another occasion, he had received a call from the New York State Police informing him that a certain Louisa Higgins had been arrested. She had no identification, but claimed to be his mother and gave them his address. They had picked her up in a liquor store, after she'd been seen slipping a bottle of whisky into a shopping bag she'd stolen a few minutes earlier from a five-and-ten.

Now, Nora was looking at him silently. He did not feel like eating any more. He had his elbows on the table and was holding his head in his hands.

"Are you crying?" she asked finally.

"No."

To prove it, he looked up, so that she could see there were no traces of tears on his face.

"She doesn't know our new address," she said, to make him feel better.

He shrugged. It wouldn't take his mother long to find it out. She might already be in town, making inquiries at the supermarket or in their old neighborhood.

They had told the children their grandmother was in a hospital, sick and infirm. Later, when each was old enough to understand, they had explained, without going into details, that she was not exactly in her right mind.

"What does she do that's so weird?" Archie had asked, amused by it all. "Does she imitate animals? Does she think she's a cow or a bear?"

Isabel did not know yet. As for Florence, her visit to Glendale had made a strong impression on her, and she had asked her father several times about Louisa.

"Are any of her brothers and sisters crazy?"

"I don't think so."

"Aren't you sure?"

"They live in Germany, and I've never known anything about them."

"So it's possible they're crazy, too?"

"Don't worry, Florence. Strictly speaking, your grandmother isn't crazy. I've had her examined by specialists. Have you ever heard of kleptomania?"

"Yes. But they don't put kleptomaniacs in mental institutions."

"Well, she isn't in a mental institution. It depends on the case. It was a choice between putting her in a rest home and letting her spend most of her life in jail."

"I think I'd rather go to jail," she had murmured, with a shiver.

How old was she when that conversation took place? It was a few days after Louisa had turned up in Williamson. Florence heard noises downstairs, got out of bed, and found her father in the kitchen with the old lady. She was fifteen.

"Is this the ugly little thing you brought to see me once?" his mother had snarled.

Now, there was nothing to do but wait. They might get a phone call any minute, or they might spend days of uncertainty, waiting for a disaster. It all depended on whether and when Louisa got hold of something to drink. If she got drunk, she would lose her natural, almost animal-like caution, and the police would soon pick her up. If, on the other hand, she stayed more or less sober, then she stood a good chance of reaching Williamson.

"Are you depressed?"

"No."

He was telling the truth. It wasn't depression he was feeling, but a much more complex emotion, one he couldn't explain to his wife, at least not now.

In a few days, he had had to re-examine everything he believed, and he had known right from the beginning that eventually he would have to confront the most important question, the one that was perhaps at the root of everything, though he had spent his whole life trying to believe the opposite.

It was time for him to go back to work. As he stood up, Nora noticed a strange glint in his eyes, which reminded her of Louisa. She got to her feet and placed both hands on his shoulders.

She stood like this for a moment, looking him straight in the face, and her lips trembled as she said, before turning away abruptly: "Think of us, Walter!"

Chapter Six

For nearly three hours, sometimes drowsing, sometimes almost completely awake, he had been aware of the life of the household going on around him. There were times when he felt as though he were spying on someone else's family through a keyhole.

When Isabel woke up the first time, sunlight was already filtering through the slits in the curtains, and, even if he hadn't known what day it was, he could have guessed it was Sunday. Perhaps it had something to do with the sounds, which were not the same as during the week, and also with a certain restfulness, a certain quality of calm that reigned over the town and the countryside. Starlings were chattering on the lawn, and twice a squirrel jumped from a branch of the nearest maple onto the roof over his head.

Isabel muttered indistinctly, then hummed, and tossed and

turned for a few minutes before falling asleep again. It was possible that Higgins had gone back to sleep, too, and was reawakened when Nora began, slowly and very carefully, to get out of bed. The rule on Sundays was to let him sleep; until he got up, the children had to creep around the house and whisper.

For a second, half opening one eye, he caught a glimpse of his wife standing naked between the bed and the window, a ray of sunlight striking her rounded belly, its navel almost invisible. A little while later, he heard the sound of running water. On Sundays, Nora always spent more time than usual in the bathroom, washing her hair. Downstairs, her comings and goings in the kitchen were different, too, and he made a game of trying to guess what she was doing from the barely perceptible sounds that reached him.

His nose tickled. He was sure now he was not going to be seriously ill, as he had hoped the previous night, but was merely starting a head cold. He was never really sick, but often suffered from stupid little ailments—colds, boils, sore throats—and sometimes he was so constipated his face turned ashen.

All the children had gone out last night except Isabel. He had told her a story in bed, then had stayed in the living room all evening with Nora, hardly speaking, waiting for the phone to ring. It had been disconcerting not to have any work to do for the school board, as he would have had if he had not resigned. He had tried to take an interest in what was on television. Then, with the set still on, he had buried himself in a magazine.

Each time a car turned the corner of Maple Street, he had jumped, but nobody had rung their bell. The house had been so quiet that, when Nora stood up to switch the TV off, it had seemed to him he could hear his heart beating.

HINSDALE PUBLIC LIBRARY
HINSDALE, ILLINOIS

At about seven this morning—he had not turned to look at the alarm clock—Isabel had gotten up, and he had heard her steps on the stairs. She was probably in her pajamas; on Sunday they all ate breakfast in their pajamas, since they all had to wait their turn to get into the bathroom, which always caused arguments. There was a special smell in the kitchen then, a smell of bed, of warm human bodies gathered together in a small space.

Nora was whispering. Isabel forgot she had to speak low; he heard her shrill voice. Dave was the next to go down, opening the door of the refrigerator and then slamming it shut, as he always did. It must be the first Sunday of fishing season. There was a constant hum of outboard motors from the lake, like the hum of the lawn mowers.

The bells of the Catholic church rang out. Now it was Archie's turn to go downstairs, half-asleep, rubbing his eyes, bumping against the wall and the banister. The smell of bacon and coffee drifted up to the second floor.

How many almost identical Sundays had he lived through in the firm belief that he was a happy man? When they were living in their old cramped house, where they could hear every noise their neighbors made, they had often said: "When we have a modern house . . ."

They were sure their life would be different, that all their troubles would vanish, just as, eighteen years before, he had stroked Nora's hand and murmured: "When we have two hundred dollars a month to spend . . ."

He tried to go back to sleep, but without success. Just before nine, when only Florence was still in bed, he got up, put on his bathrobe and slippers, and went downstairs, after glancing at himself for a moment in the mirror.

His nose was not red yet, but his eyes were brighter than

usual. On the back of his neck, he could feel the cool air coming through the half-open window.

"Can we turn the TV on, Dad?"

As expected, Nora intervened.

"You could say good morning to your father first, Archie."

"Good morning, Dad. Can I turn the TV on?"

"Your sister's still asleep."

"Hasn't she had enough sleep? I bet she's only pretending."

In other houses in the neighborhood, and in the rest of the town, things must be happening at the same rhythm as here, with the same gestures, the same words. He and Nora exchanged a glance, as if to say: Still nothing!

They were both surprised. It was more disturbing than reassuring, because it seemed to indicate that Louisa wasn't up to her usual tricks, and consequently it would take longer to track her down. The fact that she was still at large, concocting heaven knew what crazy plans, posed a constant threat, and they could do nothing to protect themselves. They could only wait and hope that she didn't show up in Williamson and create a scandal.

Nothing unusual had happened yesterday afternoon. Everything had been normal at the supermarket: customers had come and gone, greeting him and exchanging a few words as if everything was as it should be.

Yet there was something new, something unsettling, even though the business of the country club and the new school had been pushed into the background by his mother's escape.

On Saturdays, the store closed at eight o'clock, and by the time he got home, Florence was leaving. She came into the garage to get her bicycle just after he'd driven in. It was rare for them to be alone together, especially outside the house. Even inside, there was no privacy; as in most modern houses, the walls were thin, and everything could be heard from one room to the next.

"Are you going out?" he asked, to break the silence.

She stood hesitating, her hands on the handlebars.

"You know, Dad, who blackballed you?" she asked, without looking him in the face.

He shook his head.

"Bill Carney."

"Who told you that?"

"Lucille. She got it from her boss."

Lucille was Olsen's secretary. She was an unprepossessing girl; the end of her pointed nose looked as if it had been tacked on as an afterthought, and her mouth was too big and gave her face a comical expression.

"Did Olsen tell her?"

"She overheard a phone conversation."

"About me?"

It had to be about him, at least in part, if his blackballing had been mentioned.

"Did she say anything else?"

"No."

He suspected that Florence was lying to be kind. Her friend must have given her details that she did not want to tell him.

"I never thought Bill Carney liked you," she continued.

"Why?"

"No particular reason. Maybe because he feels you're different."

With that, she left.

The word "different" stuck in his mind. Bill was the only person he had never suspected of voting against him. How could he, when he was the one who had offered to propose him, apparently eagerly?

Had his mother been right all along?

"Do you really think they'll ever let the son of Louisa and that scum Higgins become one of them? . . ."

Was that what Florence meant when she uttered the word "different"? Was it because he was different that she had always looked at him with a mixture of curiosity and disapproval?

In what way was the scene in their kitchen this morning any different from what was happening in the other kitchens on Maple Street, or in the rest of what could be called the "good" neighborhood? Even the architecture of their house was copied from other houses, and their furniture was the same as Mrs. Stilwell's.

Ever since his childhood, ever since he had gone to collect his mother from the police station in Old Bridge at the age of eight, he had tried to observe other people and be like them—not the people in the neighborhood they lived in then, who were all more or less the same as him, but the kind of people everyone respected and took as models.

He must have been blind. As recently as last week, he had been convinced that he had succeeded, and that nobody could tell the difference. He himself had forgotten he was not one of them: he thought like them, behaved like them, and brought up his children the way they did.

"Two eggs, Walter?"

Sometimes he ate two eggs, sometimes only one, with his bacon. Absently, he replied: "Yes, two."

And he added, as if it were an important piece of news: "I've got a cold."

"Great! That means everyone'll get one!"

It never failed. Isabel was always the first to catch his colds, then Dave, and then Archie. Nora was always last, and it always hit her the hardest, because she developed throat complications. Only Florence remained immune. He could not remember ever having to call the doctor for her. She had not had mumps or whooping cough or chicken pox, or any other childhood disease, whereas her brothers and sister caught them one after the other, as if on an assembly line.

"I can hear her moving around, Dad."

He heard the footsteps on the second floor and gave Archie permission to turn on the television. For a few moments, as Archie turned the switch, there was the sound of an organ in a Catholic Mass, then the threatening voice of a preacher, before he finally found a children's program.

To make sure she was not kept waiting, Florence took her bath before coming downstairs. Dave quickly asked: "Can I have the bathroom next, Dad?"

"Where are you going this morning?"

"I promised Russell I'd help him fix his motorbike."

"Oh, boy, more filthy clothes!" said Nora.

They argued about it. There were invariably arguments of this kind, which ended in punishments and tears.

Higgins went out to the mailbox to get the Sunday paper, but he only glanced at the headlines. He had to wait nearly an hour before it was his turn to closet himself in the bathroom. The air was mild, the leaves on the trees were a tender green, and in the garden of the house opposite—the Wilkies were still in Florida—the automatic sprinkler switched on, and a fine spray of water was falling on a tulip bed.

Higgins shaved and dressed with the same care he used every Sunday. It did not occur to him that none of it mattered. The rituals had become part of his life, and he could not imagine behaving any differently.

"At least wash your hands and clean your shoes. They're covered with dust!"

Those words were also heard every Sunday. They meant that Dave had come back from his friend Russell's house, and that everyone downstairs was getting ready to go to the eleven o'clock service.

The Methodist church was only a mile from their house, so, since moving to Maple Street, they walked there. The children went ahead, past the front lawns, except Isabel, who sometimes slipped between her mother and father and took their hands in hers. On the opposite side of the street, in the shade of the maples, other families were making the same journey, at the same pace, and cars glided noiselessly by on the asphalt, some with golf bags, fishing equipment, or canoes on their roofs.

What would he do if he suddenly ran into his mother, or if she turned up in church during the sermon? He was sure that Nora, who was having difficulty walking and had to stop now and then to catch her breath, must be thinking the same thing, and he resented it. This was his problem and nobody else's.

Hadn't he always done what he had to to protect his wife and children? Hadn't he gone to New York to consult a psychiatrist, and then made the decision to send Louisa to Glendale? He hadn't waited for Nora to ask him. If he had made a mistake, then that, too, was his affair.

He occasionally wondered, especially when he was tired or had problems at work, whether he had done the right thing, and each time concluded that he had no reason to reproach himself.

He still thought that. He did not feel guilty about his mother. Yet he was beginning to consider things in a different light. He was on a path down which Nora could not follow him.

She knew as much about his personal life as you could communicate to another person. There were things, though— perhaps the most important things—that you were not fully aware of, that you never faced up to when you were your normal self.

But sometimes, especially when you were ill, or in the evening when the sun was going down, the world around you, apparently so well organized—the new houses, the neat lawns, the shiny cars on the road—suddenly seemed less solid, less reassuring. You looked at your own children as if they were strangers, and you thought of your work and your place in society as a delusion, even a joke.

They reached the white wooden church on one side of a small square. Families were slowly climbing the steps and disappearing into the dark interior. The Higgins family climbed them just as solemnly and were quickly bathed in coolness and silence. They took their places together, except for Florence, who for the past few months had been sitting with Lucille at the rear.

He had chosen this church himself, for no particular reason, but today, looking at the faces and backs around him, he thought he understood why. There was no sign here of the Blairs, or the Olsens, or the Holcombs, or most of the other important people in town. They all belonged to the Presbyterian church.

Just as he had discovered the geography of the town hall on the night of the meeting, now he discovered a kind of religious geography, though not without a certain bitterness.

Like his family, the other worshipers were in their Sunday best. They all had something too clean, too stiff, too well scrubbed about them. They all belonged to a certain section of the middle class. They were the sort of people who worked hard to climb one or two rungs of the social ladder, and hoped their children would climb one or two more.

Almost all of them had had a difficult start in life, and they felt reassured by the austere atmosphere of this church, where everything was simple and clean, and there was none of the pomp of the Presbyterians. They came here to find encouragement for the harsh discipline they imposed on themselves, and perhaps also to be convinced that it would not be in vain.

Most of the faces were solemn and imbued with a joyless serenity. The hymns were accompanied, not by the imposing sound of an organ, but by a meager harmonium. The minister, the Reverend Jones, was an athletic-looking man with blue eyes, who showed no indulgence toward sinners.

In a harsh voice, he preached about the God of Hosts, basing his talk on a Scriptural text. Higgins did not listen to him. Each time a latecomer crept in, he gave a start, but didn't dare turn around.

There were a few Negroes in the congregation. They were more dressed up than the others, and the women wore the brightest hats. No doubt they would have preferred to attend a Baptist service, but there was no Baptist church in the area.

The Italians, Irish, and Poles who lived downtown all belonged to the Catholic church. They had only to go and confess their sins to a priest to be absolved.

He had his money ready for the collection plate. He sang along with the others, and, by his side, Isabel sang, too, though she did not know all the words.

He was not sure he was a believer. He had adopted religion, just as he had adopted the other ideas and rules that had inspired him until now, but he had never experienced the fervor of Lucille, for instance, or Miss Carroll, who was sitting two rows away.

He had never wondered if Nora was religious. The church was part of their lives, just like the house, the school, the supermarket, and the committees he belonged to. Today, he noticed that his wife was praying fervently, moving her lips and looking straight in front of her. Had her pregnancy inspired in her a kind of mystical dread? Or was she praying that nothing would happen to them, and, above all, as she had said yesterday, that he would put his family first in the crisis he was going through?

She had sensed his uncertainty. She must be aware that it was their very existence, the existence they had patiently built up together, that was threatened.

She was right. Even now, at this very moment, standing in his pew of light oak, with his hymn book in his hand, he felt himself to be a stranger, not just to the town and the families around him, but also to his own family.

There was a rustling—the sound of books being closed, of feet on the flagstones—and he realized the service was over. They waited their turn to leave. At the top of the steps, he shook hands with the Reverend Jones, and it seemed to him that the minister held his hand longer than usual.

Jones must know about the town hall meeting and the country club affair. Was that pressure of his firm fingers a way of urging Higgins to stay in the bosom of the community? It embarrassed him, and a blush rose to his cheeks, as if someone were prying into his private life.

"Can I hire a boat this afternoon, Dad?"

Dave had joined his friends, who were walking together, waving their arms, dragging their feet. Archie had grabbed his father's hand.

"Who do you plan to go on the lake with?"

"Johnny and Phil. They've got their parents' permission. We'll each pay our share. I have the money."

He agreed without consulting his wife. He would have agreed to anything this morning.

"Me, too, Dad?" asked Isabel.

Nora intervened.

"Not you. You'll go on the lake when you can swim."

"I can swim."

"Not well enough."

"I learned last summer."

"And you'll learn some more this summer."

How many parents and children had the same conversation?

"Anyhow, the water's still too cold."

"I don't want to swim, just to take a boat ride."

"Forget it, Isabel. The answer's no."

"It's always no. Everything I ask, the answer's no."

"And don't start crying."

It all seemed so pointless! Why did they carry on so? Where did it get them? Maybe the O'Connors had the right attitude. One of them had been in church; the sixteen-year-old who had worked for him at the supermarket had just passed them on his bicycle. The rest of the family never went to church, but that one was already following the path Higgins had taken.

"What're we going to eat?" asked Archie, who was always hungry.

"Chicken."

"With mashed potatoes and peas?"

They had chicken with mashed potatoes and peas every Sunday, and beef stew every Monday. Their meals were as regulated as the rest of their lives, the same menus recurring on the same days week after week, and their conversations around the table were so similar that no thought was needed before speaking.

"At last," sighed Nora, when they got home. "It was a quiet morning."

She could not be more explicit, because of the children, but she was telling him, in a roundabout way, that they had gained time, at least.

Higgins lingered in the yard, wondering where his mother was at that moment, and resenting the fact that both he and his wife spoke of her as a threat. Where had she spent her first night as a fugitive? What condition was she in right now, in the midst of a world that didn't want her?

She had said to him: "I carried you inside me. . . ."

She had been trying to make him feel sorry for her, but it was an act. She had never been concerned about his welfare, never wondered what would become of him.

It occasionally crossed his mind that she might envy the position he had managed to attain, might envy Nora, too, and the children, and the life they led.

Had she, too, once, tried to make something of herself?

She had married Higgins. They had taken the trouble to get a license and appear before a justice of the peace. Wasn't that significant in itself? They had rented an apartment and lived there together, for however short a time.

What had been her dreams when she discovered she was pregnant with Patricia? She could have had an abortion, like so many other women. But she had accepted the idea of becoming a mother, and had let the child be born.

She had come with a friend, all the way from a working-class suburb of Hamburg, and had wandered from town to town on a new continent whose language and customs she had had to learn. What had she been searching for? Did she have no other ambition than to drink her fill and grab whatever objects came within her reach?

"I never want to be hungry again. . . ."

He had often been hungry, too, when he was left alone at the age of ten or fifteen, but he was too proud to press his nose against restaurant windows. He never wanted to be hungry again either. Above all, he never wanted to be cold again. Being cold was worse than anything. He had been cold for nights on end, so cold he thought he would die.

"Walter!"

"Yes?"

"That screw on the oven has come out again. Can you fix it?"

They had bought the new gas oven only a few months before, but one of the screws was continually coming out.

"Didn't you call Gleason?"

"He came twice, but it never seems to happen when he's here."

He went to get a tool, took off his jacket, and squatted down in front of the hot oven. The two youngest children were already watching TV.

"Did Mr. Jones say anything to you on the way out?"

"No. Why?"

"No reason."

"What could he have said?"

"I don't know.."

That was another thing to worry about. The Reverend Jones tended to get involved in the private lives of his parishioners. Higgins wondered if his wife had run into him in the past few days and confided in him, which would explain the insistent handshake.

"Has he been to see you?"

"Not since last month, when he called about the charity bazaar."

He did not ask her if she had paid him a visit. He was sure she would lie if he did. It made him think of Dr. Rodgers, who, like a minister, also devoted his life to reassuring people. An idea came to him, an idea he knew he would never do anything about. If it were not so ridiculous, or would not make him seem weak, he would like to have a real man-to-man talk with someone like Dr. Rodgers. He chose Dr. Rodgers because the man seemed so self-confident, and because through his profession he was used to listening to people's problems.

Higgins wanted to express himself without inhibition, to reveal the kind of thoughts that came to him when he was lying in bed.

"Do you really think, Doctor, that I'm a man like other men?"

The answer seemed obvious, but it was not really so clear. He would tell him everything. He would explain what his exclusion from the country club, something apparently so childish and ludicrous, really meant to him. He would talk about his mother, and about all the things he had spent his life so determinedly trying to escape from.

Hadn't he behaved rather like a small child, running as fast as his legs could carry him because he had heard footsteps in the dark and was scared?

Could there be other men in Willamson in the same situation? It was possible. He did not know everyone's past. Among the factory supervisors, the craftsmen, the small-business men, weren't there those who had known problems similar to his?

He had been told that the doctor, who was born in Providence, came from a poor family, and had had to rely on scholarships to be able to get through medical school. And his wife, again according to those in the know, had been an assistant in a five-and-ten and had continued working there for some years after they were married.

It didn't mean anything, however. Each person's case was different.

"Do you know anyone who's happy, Doctor?"

That wasn't the precise word, but he knew what he was trying to say. There was no word for what he had in mind: someone who was at peace with himself and who didn't ask himself questions, or someone who had found all the answers. No, it was more complicated than that!

He had thought he was that man—not always, not every hour of the day and night. He had had his moments of weakness and doubt, but then he would look at the goal he had set himself and get on with the job at hand.

The reason he worked every evening at jobs he didn't have to do, and that earned him nothing, was not so much because he wanted to help the community, or because he was vain enough to want a title like deputy treasurer, but because, whenever he had a few hours with nothing to do, there was such a sense of emptiness that he felt positively dizzy.

Was this the reason people rushed to the movies or switched on their TV sets as soon as they got in their front doors?

What did Nora think about all day long, alone in the house? What did she have to occupy her mind and give her a sense of importance? At least he had the bustle of the supermarket, the phone calls, the letters to be dictated and signed, as well as the deference of the staff and the good will of the customers.

"It's fixed. I hope it'll hold this time."

"Are you ready to eat?"

"Is Florence home yet?"

"I can hear her talking out on the street."

The two girls were standing on the edge of the lawn, in the sun. A moment later, Lucille headed off toward Prospect Street.

"Lunch is ready!" he called, looking in the living room. "Wash your hands."

"They aren't dirty, Dad."

"I said wash your hands."

Because it was a habit, because you had to follow the rules.

"Are you really letting him go out on the lake this afternoon?"

"Why not? The weather's mild."

"How's your cold?"

"It hasn't really started yet, but I can feel it building up."

His voice had already changed a little, and the eggs this morning had not tasted the way they usually did. It was always eggs that had a different taste when he was not feeling well.

"Where's Dave?"

"I'm here!" came Dave's loud voice.

"Where were you?"

"In the garage, pumping up my bike tires."

"Wash your hands."

"I just washed them."

"Show me."

It was true. They were still moist, because he never wiped them properly.

"I want a leg!" declared Archie.

And, as expected, his sister copied him, in a higher voice: "I want a leg, too."

He tried to imagine what it would be like if the house

disappeared and they were adrift in a no-man's-land, with no house, no gas oven, no chicken with mashed potatoes and peas.

The children, their napkins tied around their necks, were starting to eat, and Nora, after a glance to make sure she had not forgotten anything, was just sitting down with a sigh of relief, when the telephone rang. The sound seemed somehow more violent, more urgent, than on other days, and made them all jump.

Nora made no move to get up. Nor did Florence, though most calls were for her.

It was Higgins who slowly stood up, sure that the impending disaster had finally happened. He forced himself not to hurry as he headed for the living room.

"Hello!" they heard him say.

Then, with longer or shorter pauses between the words, pauses that frightened Nora, they heard: "Yes . . . Yes . . . Yes . . . Walter J. Higgins . . . That's right. I was in church an hour ago. . . ."

Nora already knew this was no ordinary call. If it had been, he would not have had to say that last sentence. Nor would he be speaking in that controlled voice, as if he wanted, at all costs, to keep calm.

"I said I was in church. . . . In church, yes . . . Can't you hear me? Can you hear me better now?"

It must be a long-distance call, which somewhat reassured Nora. It wasn't the local police, or the sheriff, or anyone in Williamson or the surrounding area.

"That's right. . . . What? . . . Sixty-eight . . . Yes, she looks older. . . . It figures. . . . I was waiting for something like this to happen. . . . I can't explain over the phone. . . . Yes . . . yes . . . I'll leave in a few minutes—as soon as I've taken the car out of the garage. . . . Yes, I'll pay the expenses. . . . What's that? . . . I don't know. . . . It's Sunday, and the roads are probably crowded. It'll take at least three hours, maybe three and a half. . . . I won't go through downtown New York. That'll save time. . . ."

Just as in a storm, when you counted the seconds between a flash of lightning and the peal of thunder, Nora was making deductions, calculations. Louisa wasn't in Glendale, because that was near the Connecticut line, and he wouldn't need more than an hour and a half to get there. Besides, he had mentioned avoiding New York, which meant that his destination was beyond that.

"Thank you, miss . . ."

It wasn't the police either, or there wouldn't have been a woman on the line.

Everyone was looking toward the door as he came back. He made an effort to appear natural, which was not difficult, because he hadn't had time to react fully. The news he had heard was still just a collection of words and had not yet translated itself into images.

"Are you leaving right away?"

He nodded.

"Where, Dad? Where are you going?"

"Don't bother your father. He has important business to attend to."

"What business?"

"Shouldn't you have something to eat first?"

"I'm not hungry."

"Take your coat. It'll be colder this evening. Do you want me to go with you?"

"You know the doctor told you not to travel by car."

"Can I go, Dad?"

"No, Archie. Don't forget you're going to the lake."

"How about me, Dad?"

"You can't go either, Isabel. You all stay here. You, too, Nora. I'll get the car out first, and then I'll be back for my coat."

They heard him opening and closing the door, then the sound of the engine starting. Through the window, they saw him stop the car, get out, bare-headed, and come back toward the house. Nora stood up.

"Not you, children. Eat your food."

"I want to say good-bye to Dad."

"He'll come and say good-bye to you all."

She got his hat and coat from the closet. When he entered, she asked: "Have you got enough money?"

"I think I have enough."

"And your checkbook?"

He felt his pocket.

"Yes."

"The children want you to kiss them good-bye."

He went around the table. As he leaned over Isabel, she began to cry, for no reason.

"I don't want you to go."

"I'll be back in time for your story."

"That's not true," retorted Archie. "You said it would take three hours or more to get there. It's farther than New York— maybe as far as Philadelphia."

"Let your father go."

Isabel clung to him, and repeated: "I don't want him to go."

He managed to get free and hurried outside. Nora followed him.

"What happened?" she asked in a low voice.

"She was hit by a bus."

"Where?"

"Just outside Old Bridge." His voice was hard, and there

was a fixed look in his eyes. It was as if these words had a particular significance for him.

"Was it the hospital that called?"

"Yes."

"Is her condition serious?"

He shrugged. "They don't know yet."

She made another deduction.

"At least she must be conscious, or she wouldn't have been able to give them your name. How did they get hold of our address?"

"They phoned our old number, and the people there told them where we live."

"Drive safely."

"Yes."

Through the open door, he could see the table with the four children sitting around it. He turned his head away.

"Aren't you going to kiss me?" she asked.

"I'm sorry."

He kissed her, and it embarrassed him, as it had earlier with the minister, that she held on to him too long.

"Be brave, Walter."

"Thank you," he murmured.

Chapter Seven

They had rerouted the highway. It no longer crossed the railroad tracks near the gasworks, but, instead, went over the marshes on a kind of causeway, and because of this he almost missed the turnoff to the town where he was born and had spent the first thirty-five years of his life.

He had been driving for about three hours, and in all that time his mind had been a blank. He had kept his eyes fixed on the white lines unraveling in front of him, while an incessant sound—of thousands of tires on asphalt—had droned in his ears.

He had followed the parkway as far as New York, and, all the way, there had been a constant stream of cars, two and sometimes three lanes of them in both directions—a movement so implacable it looked like headlong flight. Their brows furrowed, their muscles tensed, the drivers, often with whole families in the back seats, charged straight ahead as if their lives were in jeopardy, some of them not knowing where they were heading, or heading nowhere in particular, just desperately filling the empty hours with noise and speed.

Here and there, by the sides of roads that branched off the highway, were brightly colored stands selling food and drink—hot dogs, ice cream, soft drinks, coffee. And in the cars, children had ice-cream cones in their hands, and men could be seen drinking from bottles or cans.

As planned, Higgins had by-passed Manhattan and crossed the George Washington Bridge to New Jersey.

Off to his left, the skyscrapers rose, pink in the sun. Occasionally a jet tore across the clear blue sky.

Not once during the journey had he wondered if his mother was going to die, or had already died. The image that stayed with him was one he'd unconsciously carried away from Williamson: his four children, glimpsed through the open door of the kitchen, sitting around the table eating chicken.

He had to leave the highway, since it no longer went into Old Bridge, and it was not until he reached Lincoln Street that he knew where he was. There had been a lot of construction work in the last ten years, more than in Williamson, and the vacant lot where he had once played was now part of a housing development, the houses all built to the same design, the sidewalks unfinished, and the trees only half-grown.

In a rectangular space surrounded by a green fence, boys about Dave's age were playing baseball, watched by about a hundred spectators scattered on bleachers. An umpire in dark blue and a peaked cap was rushing around among the players, taking his role seriously.

Lincoln Street had not changed, but it was Sunday, so the stores were closed. There was not a soul to be seen on the sidewalks, and only a few empty cars were parked at the curbs, giving off a smell of metal roasting in the sun. In the town hall square, where two movie theaters faced each other, almost the entire parking area was filled with cars. Those people who were not sleeping or watching TV at home, with their windows open, must be at the movies, staring at screens full of outsize figures, or else on the road, like all the people he had seen since leaving Williamson.

A deathly calm seemed to lie over the town. As he drove through the empty streets, turning left, then left again, skirting sidewalks he had walked on thousands of times, he was gripped by a vague sense of dread.

He finally reached the hospital, and found that it, too, had changed. In place of the old buildings, with their barred windows and their bricks blackened by smoke from the trains that passed through the cut below, there was a modern construction of concrete and pink brick, with a broad entrance under a glass canopy, just like a luxury hotel.

It was three-thirty by the electric clock in the waiting room. The floor was white tile, the walls were white, and the furniture was new. To the left was the office, which had a sliding window in its glass wall.

From the noise that filled the corridors, and the patients he saw passing, some in wheelchairs, accompanied by spouses and children, he guessed it was visiting hour, and there to prove it was an old lady he recognized, sitting behind a table distributing pink slips to new arrivals.

So far, it was the only detail that had not changed since the days when he had come here periodically to see his mother. There was a committee of Old Bridge women who provided patients with reading matter and undertook various small tasks, including control of the comings and goings of visitors.

The one who was here today had been doing it twelve or thirteen years ago, too. She was dressed, now as then, in a white-and-violet dress and a little velvet hat adorned with a bright violet. Higgins even thought he recognized her sickly sweet smell. He did not know her name. The black limousine parked near the entrance, with a chauffeur in beige livery in the front seat, must be hers. He could have sworn she was no older than before. It was as if she had never moved from her place here in the lobby.

"Whom do you want to see?" she asked, with a candied smile.

"Mrs. Higgins, Louisa Higgins."

She looked at the list in front of her through a thick lorgnette that hung on a ribbon around her neck.

"Are you sure of the name?"

"Unless she registered under her maiden name. In that case, it's Louisa Fuchs."

"Have you been told she's here?"

"The hospital phoned me this morning in Connecticut."

"You'd better ask in the office. I can't find it. I'm sorry I can't help you."

Three well-behaved little Negro boys were sitting in armchairs, the legs of the two youngest not even touching the floor. They looked at him gravely. Higgins guessed that their mother had just given them a new brother or sister, and that they were not allowed up to the maternity ward for fear of bringing germs from the outside world.

He knocked at the closed window, and a young girl who had been reading a movie magazine slid it open.

"I've come to see my mother, Mrs. Higgins. She may be registered under her maiden name, Fuchs."

"Has she been here long?"

"Since this morning."

"One moment, please."

She also looked at a list. Then she went through some files, looked surprised, and picked up the phone.

"Do you have a patient named Higgins or Fuchs who came in this morning?"

She came back to him, shaking her head.

"There's nobody of that name listed in our admissions. Are you sure it was this hospital?"

"Is there another one in Old Bridge?"

"There's a private clinic, on the west side of town, near the park."

He knew it. It was very expensive, not the kind of place an accident victim would be taken.

"They phoned me this morning," he insisted.

"Who phoned? Do you know who it was?"

"A woman. I assume it was a nurse."

He spoke in a humble voice, without losing his patience. He was impressed by all this whiteness and neatness.

"Strictly speaking," the girl explained, "the office is closed on Sunday. The director isn't here. There's just me on duty. The girl who was on duty this morning has already left. What time did she call?"

"Just after noon."

"I came on duty at one."

His hands were sweaty, and he wanted to blow his nose.

"Is it for an operation?"

"I guess so. They said there'd been an accident."

Just then, a nurse came into the office. The contours of her body could be made out beneath her uniform, especially when she stood in front of the window.

"Do you have a cigarette?" she asked the girl, taking no notice of Higgins.

"There's a pack in my purse. Take it. I have another in

the drawer. Do you know anything about an accident victim brought in this morning?"

"Oh, the old . . ." She saw Higgins and stopped abruptly, embarrassed. "The one who was hit by a bus?" she asked.

"Yes," he said quickly.

"Is she here?" asked the secretary, surprised. "Why isn't her name on the admissions list?"

"I have nothing to do with that. All I know is she came in by ambulance."

"What ward is she in?" he asked.

For them, it was an ordinary conversation, the kind they had every day. The nurse turned to Higgins. Once again, she seemed to hesitate.

"I don't think she's in a ward. They took her straight to Emergency."

The secretary explained.

"That means you can't see her yet. Visitors aren't allowed in Emergency."

"But they phoned me . . ."

"I know."

Maybe she was new, or sitting in for someone and was afraid to assume responsibility. Her uniformed friend, who had red hair like Florence's, leaned over and whispered something in her ear.

"Well, if you think so . . ."

The nurse came out of the office, though not before slipping the pack of cigarettes into the pocket of her uniform.

"Come with me," she said to Higgins. "It's against the rules, but we'll see what the head nurse says."

"Is she the one who phoned me?"

"No, not Mrs. Brown—that's for sure. She didn't come on duty till one, like everyone else. Follow me."

After a brief exchange with the woman in the hat with the

violet, who raised no objection, she led him down a series
of corridors. Through half-open doors he could see patients
lying in bed, surrounded by visitors who had brought flow-
ers, candy, or fruit. A little boy of five, about the same height
as Isabel, passed them on crutches, his right leg almost hor-
izontal in front of him.

They came to a kind of crossroad, where there was an
information board above a desk. A doctor was looking through
the nurses' reports, and two nurses were putting glasses of
fruit juice on large trays.

"This way . . ."

She pushed open a door with a NO ENTRY sign on it. Beyond, all was quiet. There seemed to be nobody in the corridor or in the adjoining rooms, which were filled with strange
instruments.

"Mrs. Brown!" she called, in a low voice.

Getting no reply, she called again.

"Mrs. Brown!"

Finally, she said to Higgins: "Wait here."

A little way down the corridor, she opened a door with a
red light above it and closed it behind her.

More than ten minutes went by. Although Higgins was
bathed in sweat, and his shirt was sticking to his back, he
did not dare take off his coat.

His mind was still blank. This place seemed detached from
the world, almost as if it were not part of real life. Birth,
pain, death: none of these things had the same meaning here
as elsewhere. He had been as shocked, earlier, to see the
nurse's long legs silhouetted against the light as he would
have been had he seen the same thing in church, and he
had been equally shocked that she had made sure she brought
her cigarettes with her.

A badly shaved man of indeterminate age, dressed in striped

cotton and carrying a bucket and a broom, suddenly emerged from a staircase that Higgins had not noticed and eyed him suspiciously.

"Are you the new doctor?"

"No."

"Then what are you doing here?"

"A nurse told me to wait and went into that room."

He pointed to the door with the red light, and the man walked away, shaking his head and muttering indistinctly.

Perhaps because of the pervasive smell of ether, Higgins was beginning to feel weak in the knees, but there was no chair, nowhere to sit. He did not look at his watch. It made no difference what time it was. Time had ceased to matter.

The door finally opened, and a stony-faced woman of about fifty, in a nurse's uniform, came out and stood looking at him, then walked toward him. The young nurse, who had followed her out, merely gestured discreetly at Higgins and vanished the way they had come.

"Are you Walter J. Higgins?" asked the head nurse. She had an index card in her hand.

"Yes."

"And Louisa Fuchs is your mother? It's you my colleague phoned this morning in Williamson, Connecticut?"

"Yes."

He was too overwhelmed by what was happening to ask her any questions.

"I assume your mother didn't live with you?"

"No."

"Did she live alone?"

"She lived in a rest home in Glendale."

"Dr. Andersen's rest home?"

"That's right."

"Insane?"

126

"The doctors thought she'd be better off there."

"Did she escape?"

He had still not been asked to sit down. He tried to figure out what was going on behind the door, which was still slightly ajar.

"You'll have to come to my office later for the papers. And the police want to see you. They need some information."

He asked, surprised that his voice sounded so natural: "Is she dead?"

"You didn't know?"

"No."

He had no idea if he was moved or not. All he wanted was to sit down, even if only for a moment.

"I thought they phoned you."

"Yes, but they didn't tell me she was dead. They said it wasn't yet possible to . . ."

She looked at the index card.

"She died at twelve-twenty-five."

That was just as he was leaving the house, after a last look at the children around the table.

"Did she say anything?"

"I wasn't here. If you'd like to wait a few minutes, Dr. Hutchinson will soon be out of the operating room. He was on duty when it happened. . . . Ah, here he is."

A tall young man appeared in the corridor. He had a surgeon's cap on his head, rubber gloves on his hands, and red rubber boots on his feet. He dropped the mask that covered the lower part of his face. His forehead was streaming with perspiration, and his eyes were feverish with exhaustion.

"Well?" the head nurse asked him.

"She has every chance of recovery. I'll be up to see her in an hour."

They were not talking about Louisa, but about a young

girl who was wheeled by, unconscious, on a gurney. All Higgins could see of her was her dark, silky hair, which reminded him of Nora's, and her pinched nostrils. Her thin body looked like a sculpted figure under the white sheet. She was wheeled into an elevator as Mrs. Brown explained to the doctor:

"This is the son of the woman who died at twelve-twenty-five."

Dr. Hutchinson had gone into a bathroom and taken off his gloves. He washed his hands, wiped his face on the wet towel, lit a cigarette, and puffed at it greedily, all the while shooting inquisitive glances at Higgins.

"Apparently, she escaped from the rest home in Glendale," the head nurse continued.

"Was she a drinker?" the doctor asked Higgins.

"Yes."

"I thought as much. She reeked of alcohol. She must have blacked out crossing the street. That's the likeliest explanation. If it wasn't a blackout, the only other possibility is suicide."

Higgins asked mechanically: "Why?"

"Because, according to the police, apart from that bus there was no traffic on East 32nd Street, and that's quite a wide street."

They had given him the wrong information this morning, telling him the accident had happened just outside town. Or maybe the nurse who phoned considered that the town was only the shopping streets and the better neighborhoods. East 32nd Street was the street where he was born, in the barracklike building where Louisa had lived with her husband in the early days of their marriage.

"Was she in pain?" he asked, not having any clear idea what he was saying.

"She was certainly in pain when they brought her in, but she didn't let it show. You couldn't exactly say she was smiling, and yet . . ."

That sounded like Louisa. Defiant to the end.

"I sedated her almost immediately and . . ."

"Do you mean she was conscious?"

"When she came in, yes. The policeman who was with her wrote down the name she gave him."

"Mine."

"I guess so, since you're here."

From the way the doctor was staring at him, and from a certain deliberate coolness in his manner, Higgins sensed that something was still bothering him.

"What were her injuries?"

"Fractures of the cranium, left shoulder, pelvis. She lost a lot of blood. I tried a transfusion, but it was too late."

"Did she say anything?"

"Only your name and where you lived. If you like, you can have her clothes. Anything else, purse or personal effects, you'll find at the police station. I guess you need him now, Mrs. Brown?"

"Yes, Doctor."

"Can I see her?" asked Higgins.

They looked at each other. The doctor shrugged.

"Come with me," said the head nurse.

They descended a staircase to a lighted basement. Here, too, there was a corridor with doors on either side. Mrs. Brown opened one of the doors and stepped aside. The room was narrow, the walls bare. On a table that looked as if it were made of marble lay a human form covered by a white sheet. It was colder here than elsewhere.

The head nurse walked to the table and pulled the sheet back enough to show the head. It was covered with a bandage, from which little wisps of gray hair peeped out. The cheeks were partly hidden by another band of cloth, there to keep the jaws closed. So all that could be seen of the face were the sunken eyes, the narrow, pointed nose, and the colorless lips.

He did not pray, did not cry, did not dare touch the dead woman. Suddenly he felt cold, as cold as on those nights in his childhood when he was alone and could not get warm. He was afraid, too, for no very precise reason, and he looked at the head nurse for reassurance.

"Is it she?" the nurse asked.

He nodded. It was impossible for him to speak just yet. He wanted to leave this room as quickly as possible, but he felt rooted to the spot.

"Come to the office now, and tell me what you plan to do."

On the way out, she switched the light off, which startled him.

"This way."

The same girl was in the office, and in the waiting room the three little Negro boys were still in their place.

"Are you claiming the body?"

"Yes."

"Form C, Eleanor," she ordered the girl. "I assume you want the body sent to Williamson?"

He shook his head. "I'd prefer to bury her in Old Bridge. She spent most of her life here."

"That's up to you. You'll pay, of course?"

"Of course."

"In that case, you'll have to find an undertaker. Do you know one?"

"I was born here."

She frowned, as if searching in her memory, but she could

not recall him, any more than he could recall her. They had certainly not lived in the same neighborhood.

He answered all the questions he was asked. There were more comings and goings, and a few phone calls, before they finally worked out the amount he owed. He wrote a check.

When he left the hospital, he was so dazzled by the bright sunlight that it took him a while to spot his car among the other parked cars. It did not occur to him to phone Nora and tell her his mother had died. Williamson was far from his thoughts, as if he had never set foot there. Nor did his children enter his mind. He was in a strange world, a world he did not recognize, stranded between the past and the present.

Somehow, by following his nose, he found the police station. The door had not changed, but the walls inside had been repainted. The two policemen in uniform were new— they were both younger than he—but the plainclothes sergeant sitting in his shirt sleeves with a green eyeshade on his forehead, typing and chomping on a cigar, seemed familiar.

Higgins told them who he was and why he had come, and the three of them let him have his say without interruption. Then the sergeant inserted a printed form into the typewriter and began asking him questions: first name, last name, address, profession, mother's name, date of birth . . .

"How do you spell Altona?"

He told him.

"I guess you're aware we have quite a record on her?"

"Yes, I'm aware of that."

"Where do you work?"

"I'm manager of the Fairfax Supermarket, in Williamson."

"Is that the same chain as the one here?"

"I started out in the Old Bridge branch."

"Are you claiming the body?"

"Yes. I'm taking care of her funeral."

"In Williamson?"

"No. Here."

Everyone seemed to find that odd; he had no idea why.

"There'll be something to pay. We found two small bottles in her shopping bag. They came from Baumann's. We checked there. The bottles were stolen."

"I'll pay."

"Pass me the bag, Fred."

One of the officers brought him a bag made of shiny black material. The sergeant took from it a half-full bottle of gin. The other bottle lay smashed to pieces at the bottom of the bag, which still gave off a strong odor. There were also two oranges, some squashed bananas, and a package of cookies, soggy from the gin.

"That's all we found. No pocketbook. No money."

"Did you find out how she got here from Glendale?"

"Not on foot, that's for sure. Either she had enough to take the bus or she hitchhiked."

"What time was the accident?"

"Ten o'clock."

"You say she went to Baumann's. That must have been yesterday."

"They're open till ten on Saturdays."

"I know. I wonder where she spent the night."

The sergeant made a gesture that clearly meant it was no business of his.

"Sign here, in the bottom left-hand corner. Here's a receipt for the eight dollars, fifty cents. I'll see Baumann gets it."

Higgins knew that behind the office was a corridor, and

along the corridor a cell where his mother had often spent the night. But not last night.

"Are you going to the undertaker's? Which one are you using?"

"Oward and Turner, if they're still around."

There had been a Turner at high school with him. He was three years younger, and they were not friends.

"I don't suppose she said anything to the officer who picked her up?"

"The one who took her to the hospital isn't here, but he didn't mention anything in his report."

"Thanks."

"You're welcome."

For no particular reason, he was sure they would burst out laughing as soon as his back was turned. He was not walking or talking normally. He felt different, older, detached from everything, and barely recognized his surroundings. Oward and Turner had moved; they were now up on the hill, in the residential neighborhood, which had expanded without losing its character.

It was only in the old parts of towns, the poor parts, that things never changed; the streets and stores stayed the same, the houses shrank a little more each year, like old people, and the alleys still swarmed with gangs of kids.

He did not know what to say when they asked him what day he wanted the funeral to take place. It had not occurred to him that he would have to come back to Old Bridge—or, indeed, that he would have to leave it. He had lost his moorings. The future was uncertain. He was adrift in an unfamiliar world.

"Would Tuesday be convenient?"

He accepted Tuesday, unable to think.

"Ten o'clock?"

Why not? He was shown catalogues with photographs of coffins and tombstones, and a map of the nearest cemetery. It was not the one he knew, which was now full, but a new one six miles from town.

"Will you be paying now? Most people . . ."

He wrote another check. None of it mattered.

"Can you leave us your phone number? We may need to get in touch with you."

He gave his Williamson number. The man seemed surprised, just as all the others had been surprised, by Higgins's behavior.

He nearly forgot his car. He set off down the gently sloping street, from which there was a view over the rooftops of the town. He had occasionally been down this street in the past, but now it was as alien to him as everything else. Yet he could have put a name to most of the houses, thanks to the years he had spent as a delivery man. There were certain customers who always tipped him, and others who gave him Christmas presents, especially cartons of cigarettes, unaware that he did not smoke.

Shouldn't he get back on the road to New York and Connecticut? He had no idea. He needed someone to advise him, someone who knew what he wanted better than he himself did. He let his car glide down the hill, then drove through the shopping center. Outside the Fairfax Supermarket, a banner announced a promotional sale starting tomorrow, the same sale they had been having in Williamson. Abruptly, he pulled in to the curb on a corner of 32nd Street and got out.

There, barely five hundred yards away, amid the peeling and colorless buildings, was the house where he was born and where he had spent his earliest years. Although the stores were closed and shuttered, he recognized them; the names on some of them were the same as in his childhood.

Music drifted from the open windows on upper floors. Here and there, people were leaning out. At one window, a young couple stood embracing, and the outline of a big brass bed could be glimpsed in the half-light behind them.

They had not told him the exact spot along the street where the accident had taken place, and he had not dared ask. Or maybe it had not crossed his mind before. He was about to question a big woman in a red dress sitting on a chair beside her doorstep, but there was no need. A little farther on he noticed broken glass near the curb. One of the bus windows must have been smashed, maybe because a passenger had been thrown against it by the impact.

Going closer, he saw stains on the ground, brown, with a little purple where they had not dried as much. He was opposite Number 67, his childhood home. Most of the windows were without curtains, as if the occupants had fled. The door was open on a dark, cold-looking hallway.

He looked up at the two windows on the fourth floor, and again he was afraid. He had the feeling that he was in danger, and he was seized by an insane desire to turn and run away as fast as he could.

His gaze, wandering over the front of the building, slowly descended and came to rest on the second floor, where a man, his shirt sleeves rolled up, stood smoking a cigarette and watching him.

They looked at each other, and both frowned, almost at the same time. Higgins did not dare move. The man, in his frame of gray cement, suddenly broke out of his inertia, like a figure in a painting coming to life, and waved eagerly.

"Hey, Walter!"

Higgins recognized him, too. They were the same age,

had lived in this building as children, and had gone to school together. Because of his long trunk and short legs, the man had been nicknamed Shorty. Higgins could not immediately remember his real name, and, as if it were suddenly of the greatest importance, this annoyed him.

"It *is* you, Walter?" cried Shorty, who was almost completely bald, though he had a close-cropped blond mustache. "Come on up! Do you remember the way?"

A foreign name. Rader! All that was missing was the first name. Nobody had ever used it, they all called him Shorty.

Higgins did not dare refuse the invitation. A woman appeared behind his old friend's shoulder and looked in his direction. She whispered something to her husband, and he replied in a low voice.

Higgins gestured that he was coming. Head down, he crossed the street, just as his mother had that morning.

But in his case, there was no bus to hit him. Resigned to his fate, he entered the building.

Chapter Eight

Twice he nearly phoned Nora, not to put his mind at ease but to ask her to come and get him. He felt so helpless that he even considered calling Dr. Rodgers. Maybe he wasn't ill in the strict sense of the word, but wasn't this condition worse than angina or pneumonia? Wasn't it a matter of life and death? Why shouldn't there be people you could turn to for help in cases like this?

The thing he had forgotten about the old house was the smell, which caught him by the throat as soon as he started up the stairs. Maybe it hadn't been so disgusting when he was a child, or maybe he hadn't been so aware of it then because he was used to it. He was already starting to resent the fact that Rader was forcing him to make a kind of pilgrimage, and at a time when he most needed to keep a clear head.

"Come on in! It's really great to see you again. Do you know Yvonne?"

It was the woman he had seen at the window. Her hair was disheveled, and her blouse had two buttons missing, giving a glimpse of her pale, flabby breasts. She was not wearing stockings, and her ankles were dirty above her slippers.

She did not seem as happy to see him as her husband was. Sullenly, she went over to the antiquated TV set and switched off a basketball game.

"I was wondering who that guy was who was looking the building up and down, like he was planning to rent an apartment, and then I realized it was you."

Rader was talking with an enthusiasm that embarrassed Higgins; it grated on his nerves like Louisa's laughter. Later, it occurred to him that his old friend might have been doing it on purpose, just like Louisa, to annoy him or hurt him.

Rader had not shaved today, and had probably not washed either. The apartment was dirty and untidy.

"Good old Walter! Sit down, and we'll have a drink to celebrate."

Why, for once, did he not dare admit that he didn't drink? The round table was covered with oilcloth, which had several holes in it and a design that was almost worn away. Proudly, Shorty placed a bottle of Chianti and some thick, gray-looking glasses on the table.

"I've often wondered what became of you. It's not every day you run into old friends. They must be scattered all over the country. Not to mention the ones who've died. Cheers!"

His wife took one of the glasses. The wine was dark, almost black. The first mouthful Higgins took burned his throat, and he almost spat it out.

"Great stuff! Wine and spaghetti are the two best things we got from the Italians. Talking of Italians, do you remember Alfonsi? Believe it or not, he's become a priest. He's just come back to Old Bridge. Has a parish here now. It's strange when you think of the way he used to be—taking girls behind the garbage cans in the alley."

Why did he have to talk so much, without pause? The room they were in, which looked out on the street, was a combined kitchen, dining room, and living room. A stew was cooking on low heat on the gas stove. The furniture was the kind you saw in unfrequented secondhand stores.

Yet it was almost an exact replica of the room in which Higgins had spent his childhood, except that in his room there had been a metal bed in the corner, which was folded up during the day.

The Raders' bedroom door was open, and Higgins noticed the washstand with running water. In his day, they had had to get water at the end of the hallway. The two beds were unmade—maybe they had not been made for days. One of them was a very high double bed made of dark wood; the other, simply a box mattress on four blocks of wood, had dubious-looking sheets and a greenish blanket.

"I can't say you're looking well, but I guess you're prospering."

Rader seemed to size up the quality of Higgins's suit and shoes at a glance.

"I can't complain, either," he continued. "Isn't that right, Yvonne?"

Yvonne was leaning on her elbows at the window. She turned her head sulkily, almost aggressively.

"What?"

"I said we can't complain."

"What about?"

"The way we live. We don't work too hard and we eat like pigs."

She shrugged and turned back to the street.

"Were you still in Old Bridge when my mother died?"

Higgins could not remember. He had never been close to Rader, except as a boy, and when they moved after one of Louisa's disappearances, he had lost touch with him. But Rader seemed to think they had been like brothers all their lives. He refilled the three glasses.

"Cheers! What was I saying? Oh, yes! When my mother died, the old man decided he'd had enough of town and went to live with his brother-in-law in the country, in South Carolina. I kept the apartment. Hell, I think Yvonne and me'll be the last ones left in this place. It's three years since they decided to knock it down, but they haven't even started yet. God knows when they will. Half the tenants have gone. Just imagine! Your place is empty. People took the doors for firewood."

Higgins lifted his glass. The wine seemed less sickening now. He felt an unaccustomed warmth in his veins. Was his head spinning? He knew his vision was not as clear. He told himself it was his cold that was making his eyes water.

"Have any children?"

Higgins nodded, embarrassed to talk about them here.

"We've got one, too. A son. He's in the Navy. Remind me to show you his picture. He's a big boy, a whole head taller than me. We had an empty bed when he left, so I suggested to a friend of mine, who's a widower and doesn't have a soul in the world, that he come and live with us. You won't see him. Every Sunday, he goes to the bar on the corner and gets loaded. He won't get back till the middle of the night."

Higgins was still wondering whether Rader was doing this on purpose, or whether he simply didn't realize.

"As for me, my first job was at the gasworks. Then I found

something that really suits me. I drive a garbage truck. It seems disgusting when you start, but you get used to it. It isn't tiring, you do the same round every day, and the pay's good. The only drag is having to get up early in the morning."

Higgins suddenly remembered that Rader's father had been a night watchman for the railroad. He always had red eyes, because the noise in the building kept him awake during the day. They would often see him rush out of the apartment in his nightshirt, his feet bare and his hair flying, and throw the first object he could find at the kids screaming on the stairs.

Rader talked for more than an hour about the past, about people, some of whom Higgins had forgotten, but others he remembered well, like Gonzales, whose father worked at the lime kiln during the winter, then took the whole family south for the cotton-picking season.

"You knew him, too, didn't you? Wasn't he the one who beat you up that time, and you couldn't go to school for three days after?"

Higgins did not remember that. Maybe Rader was confusing him with another kid in the neighborhood.

"Did you see his name in the papers? Even the New York papers wrote about it, and showed his picture. Not our Gonzales, one of his sons. He went to work in Philadelphia when he was seventeen, and one fine day we heard he'd killed a cop. They sentenced him to death. The day he got the chair, his father, our Gonzales, cut his throat with a razor. Have some more wine!"

Higgins was beginning to feel really sick, but didn't dare say no.

"We can see everything from here. Just this morning, for instance, an old woman, a wino, threw herself under a bus. Believe me, it wasn't a pretty sight. I was at the window. I saw it all as clearly as I see you now. . . . How's life treating you?"

What could he say?

"Where do you live?"

"Connecticut."

"Plenty of rich folk there. I've never been any farther north than the city. If I had my choice, I'd rather go south, for the sun. . . . Hey, Yvonne, how about inviting Walter to stay for dinner?"

"It won't be ready for an hour," she objected.

"I have to leave before then."

"Have you got a car?"

"Yes."

"Where's it parked?"

"At the corner."

"So you came back to see the old place again? I'll tell you something I think you'll understand, though nobody else would. I love this old dump. When the time comes for me to go, I'm going to miss it."

Higgins tried hard to smile politely, but he felt sicker than ever. His stomach was heaving, and he felt like all his blood was draining from his veins.

He wanted to escape, to escape once and for all, to escape from his mother, Rader, the house, the street, everything that seemed to be conspiring to keep him here. Maybe his old friend had lied, or had made a mistake, and Louisa had not thrown herself under the bus, maybe she'd had a blackout, as the doctor had suggested. Yet now that he was here, it seemed to him she was quite capable of having done it on purpose, to force him to come back.

"No, don't go yet! One more glass and then you can go. Do you want one, Yvonne?"

What did the couple do all day besides looking out at the

street, watching TV, eating, or lying stretched out on the unmade bed?

He must not let himself get pulled down. He could feel it happening. It was then that he thought, for the first time, of phoning Nora, if only to hear her voice and make sure that she and the children and their house really existed.

His whole being protested against this past that was trying to trap him.

"Look, Shorty, I have to . . ."

"Did you hear that, Yvonne? He called me Shorty, just like he used to!"

On the stairs, as Higgins was finally getting free, Rader said: "Don't you want to go up and take a look at your old apartment?"

Higgins looked at him in terror, and had to make an effort not to fly down the stairs. Back on the street, he was so upset, so miserable, he felt like just sitting on a doorstep to wait for fate to do as it would with him. Earlier—he couldn't remember when—he had felt old. Now he felt like a child, a child who needed help. Nobody had ever helped him. Nobody! When he was still small, he had been forced to play a man's part, and he had done it, bravely.

He didn't know what to do now. He was totally at sea. Dr. Rodgers, who was an educated and experienced man, would surely come if he called him. But he didn't dare. What would the doctor think if he phoned him and said: "I'm in Old Bridge, sitting on a doorstep on 32nd Street, and I can't go on, I don't know what to do. You must come and help me."

He had stood up and challenged the people of Williamson, and he was sure they resented it. He no longer believed in them, or in anyone or anything. Yet it was impossible for him to stay here, in this town he had left behind.

He had a bad taste in his mouth, his legs felt weak, and

his movements were less than steady. He stumbled twice on the sidewalk before he reached his car. Then he had trouble getting the key in the lock.

He *had* to get away as quickly as possible, to get home and find something real to hold on to. Because of the new highway, he took a wrong turn again on the way out of town, and for a quarter of an hour went around in circles. Drivers he passed made angry gestures at him. Then he found himself driving the wrong way down a one-way street.

He drove without paying attention, until he almost hit a truck. After that, seized with fear, he slowed down. By the time night fell, he had still not reached the George Washington Bridge. He remembered he hadn't eaten anything at noon, so perhaps the sick feeling might be nothing but hunger.

The restaurants along the highway, however, made him nervous. He wasn't in the habit of stopping in such places. He passed about ten before finally turning off into a parking lot.

He was more and more certain that Rader had done it on purpose. His mother, too. It was quite vague in his mind, but he knew what he meant, and a bitter smile rose to his lips, the smile of a victim. Inside the restaurant, the tables, covered with checked tablecloths, were all occupied, and there were men at the bar and a strong smell of alcohol.

Wouldn't a glass of whisky do him good, in the state he was in? The doctor had once made Nora take some after she'd fainted. They had kept the bottle in the closet for a long time before finally throwing it away.

Why not call her? He saw a phone booth next to the rest rooms.

"What'll it be?" asked the barman. "Scotch, bourbon, or rye?"

He ordered rye, not knowing the difference, drank the contents of the little glass that was placed in front of him, then the glass of ice water he was given at the same time. Almost at once, he felt the same warmth in his body as he had felt in Rader's apartment.

Maybe that was the solution, after all. Let fate decide for him. He had struggled long enough by himself. Now he could afford to sit down by the side of the road and wait for someone to give him a helping hand.

That was just a manner of speaking. He wasn't really going to sit down by the side of the road. He'd go home, but only to go to bed. He'd say nothing to Nora. Let her take care of herself. He'd carried them all on his back long enough, and he was tired of it.

Had Rader recognized Louisa this morning? If so, everything he'd said was just play-acting. He couldn't really be satisfied with his life; it was only a crude caricature of living. Yet he seemed proud of his son in the Navy, and proud of being able to eat his fill.

". . . like pigs!" he'd said.

He clung to that hideous building, which stank of all the bad things in the world.

"Another?"

He said yes. He had to say yes. His glass was refilled from a bottle with a metal pouring lip. After that, things got hazy.

Dogged by a sense of fear and urgency, he knew he had to get back to Williamson as quickly as possible, to be out of danger. He wasn't clear what the danger was, but he was sure it existed. The trouble was, he found it difficult to control his car, and the headlights that loomed out of the night toward him were terrifying.

He bypassed New York and drove along a lighted highway that seemed to contain all the cars in the country.

He didn't want to have an accident. He didn't want them to take him to a hospital, lock him in a little basement room and turn out the light.

He could still stop and phone Nora and beg her to come to his rescue. She'd be able to borrow a car from someone, from . . .

No! Not from Bill Carney. The thought showed him how stupid he'd been. Where, then, could she get a car?

What was the good of trying to think? His head ached too much. When the highway forked, he chose the wrong way again, and drove for nearly an hour toward Albany, without knowing why the road seemed unfamiliar.

Then he saw an inn like a log cabin, like Lincoln's birthplace, and went in to ask for directions. It was hot inside. He had another drink. Then, once more, there was the night and the headlights bearing down on him, some of them blinking on and off, as if sending a message he no longer understood.

They hadn't tricked him only in Williamson. Right from his childhood, from the day he was born, everyone had tricked him, everyone without exception, starting with his mother.

He mustn't speak ill of her. She was dead, and it wasn't right to blame the dead. But he wasn't speaking, he was only thinking.

His car felt awkard on the curves, and had a tendency to veer too far to the right.

He must be cautious. That was absolutely essential. Ab-so-lute-ly. And it was essential, too, not to miss the exit to Williamson.

The dashboard clock must be wrong. It said something after midnight, and it couldn't possibly be that late. An overpowering need forced him to stop. He tried to vomit, but couldn't. He sat on the grass for a while, watching the cars flash by.

It was one-thirty in the morning when Nora, who had finally gone to bed, leaving a light on over the front door, heard the sound of brakes outside. She went to the window, parted the curtains, and saw their car parked by the curb. Surprisingly, she didn't see her husband getting out.

She threw on her dressing gown and slippers and rushed out. Through the car window, she saw her husband's face in the darkness. He was sitting as he usually did when he drove, his head upright, his hands on the wheel.

He did not turn toward her.

"Walter!"

Still he did not move. She opened the door. Getting out, he swayed so much, she thought he was going to collapse to the sidewalk.

"What's the matter? What happened?"

He looked at her without seeing her. The car smelled of alcohol.

"Have you been drinking? Do you feel sick?"

He tried in vain to speak. He opened and closed his mouth like a fish, but no sound came out. He tried to put a foot on the ground, fell, and gave a little laugh.

She was not strong enough to carry him. When he made no effort to stand up, she was forced to go in the house and wake Florence and Dave.

"Shh! Don't make a noise. Just follow me."

"What is it, Mom?" asked Isabel, half-awake, from her room.

"Nothing. Go to sleep."

Outside, Dave rubbed his eyes and asked: "What's wrong with Dad?"

"Come on, you two! Let's get him to bed."

Chapter Nine

Higgins stayed in bed for five days, and it was only when he was alone that he allowed himself to smile. Once, when he was sitting up and looking at himself in the mirror, with that smile on his face, he was struck by his resemblance to Louisa.

When he opened his eyes the first time and saw by the alarm clock that it was after noon, he felt so ashamed that he closed his eyes immediately and tried hard to go back to sleep. And, in fact, he fell asleep.

When, later, Nora brought him coffee, he stammered: "I'm sorry."

And added, by way of excuse: "My mother's dead."

"I know. I phoned the hospital in Old Bridge."

"I'm sick, Nora."

"I also phoned the doctor. He'll be along to see you at four. That's why I woke you."

He really was sick. Because of that, they were not angry with him, or if they were, they didn't show it and spoke to him gently. His pulse was irregular—sometimes rapid, sometimes too slow. From time to time, he had chest spasms that were so severe he was sure he was going to die.

He resigned himself to it. Maybe that was the best solution of all. He anticipated his death with serenity, almost with pleasure, imagining the details of the funeral and the attitudes of the people following his coffin. Wouldn't they feel sorry they'd refused him his last wish, by closing the doors of the country club to him?

At other times, later, when the pills Dr. Rodgers prescribed took effect, he felt good. His body and mind would become drowsy, though not enough for him to lose consciousness.

All in all, things had worked out better than he expected, except for the humiliation of being carried to bed by Florence and Dave.

"How did I get here?" he asked his wife.

"You parked outside and didn't move."

"Who brought me in?"

She told him.

"Did they say anything?"

"They were upset, a little scared."

"Florence, too?"

It pleased him that his daughter had been worried about him.

"Since I had no idea what had happened, I called Old Bridge."

Because of his poor health, he did not have to go back there for his mother's funeral. That made him smile, too, as if he were getting his own back on Louisa.

"How are they managing at the store?"

"Miss Carroll phoned Hartford, and they sent a replacement."

"Who?"

"I don't remember his name."

"What's he look like?"

"A little brown man, quite fat."

"Patel. I know him."

His condition must be serious, since Dr. Rodgers came to see him twice a day. If only Nora would leave them alone together, he could ask him the question he had been meaning to ask.

Was there any point now? He knew that such a thing was not done, that there were things it was better not to talk about. The only result might be to shock the doctor, but maybe the doctor already understood.

Lying in bed, he had time to get things clear in his mind, especially after the headaches and nausea of the first few days finally eased. As he did on Sunday mornings, he would listen to the sounds of the house, the street, the town, and thanks to the pills, they all formed a kind of reassuring music in his head.

The only question he asked the doctor was: "Is my heart still okay?"

"Provided you don't do it again," Rodgers replied, without a trace of severity or reproach.

Little by little, that sentence came to apply not only to drinking but also to many things. At last, he thought he could understand why Bill Carney had voted against him. And when he did, he could not blame him or bear a grudge against him.

He didn't have all the details worked out yet, but he was sure he was on the right track. The reason people thought he didn't count was because he didn't know the rules of the game. Yes, it was a game—like the games of his childhood. He hadn't known that, maybe because he'd had to start too young, or too low, he, the son, as his mother said sarcastically, of Louisa and that scum Higgins.

But that wasn't the main thing. What was important was to conform to the rules, certainly, but, most of all, to know it was all a game. If you didn't know that, you could make things impossible for other people.

Take Dr. Rodgers, for instance. It was highly unlikely that he believed in half the remedies he prescribed. He might know perfectly well that a patient he spoke to so optimistically had less than a month to live. But he couldn't tell him that. He had to inspire confidence. Just as Bill had to let people think he had been elected to the state Senate because of his devotion to the community.

Even Oscar Blair, apparently so self-confident, but in reality burdened with insoluble problems, owed it to everyone to be the very image of prosperity and success. If he were happy with his wife and all her committees, he wouldn't need to run after the three-times-divorced Mrs. Lancaster, with whom he'd had two children he couldn't acknowledge as his own. What happened when he got home? What would he tell the children when they were older? Why did he drink all day long?

It had taken Higgins a long time to reach this point. He had been naïve. He had discovered only a tiny fraction of the truth, and it had made him rise in revolt against them.

Would he really rather go back and live in that barracks he had grown up in, like his old friend Rader? It had almost happened, and he still shivered at the thought.

No. He was determined now to do everything they asked him. He was even prepared to apologize for the incident in the town hall. The fact that his mother had died, and that he had been ill after he returned, would make things easier. A notice had appeared on Wednesday in the local weekly paper, announcing that Mrs. Louisa Higgins, born Fuchs, "the mother of our distinguished fellow citizen Walter J. Higgins," had passed away the previous Sunday in Old Bridge, New Jersey, "following an accident," and that Higgins had suffered a nervous breakdown as a result of the shock.

It was possible the newspaper knew the facts about Louisa. They must have phoned the hospital, and maybe the police. Yet they didn't feel the need to print the truth. They, too, were following the rules of the game. Even about him, they were discreet.

He wasn't proud of the decision he had made. Sometimes, he felt ashamed. He would feel that way again—just as he would feel, at times, a bitter sensation of loneliness, of being in a void.

The decision was necessary. It was the price he had to pay. He had no choice. No one had a choice. He was sure that when he looked at Dr. Rodgers in a certain way, the doctor understood that he had changed. It was almost as if the two of them had winked at each other.

Was this what they called "becoming a man"? If it was, then up to the age of forty-five he had stayed a child.

"How are you, Dad?"

They took turns coming up to see him, at different times during the day. Isabel always looked at him curiously, because she was not used to his being in bed all the time.

"Are you sick?"

"No."

"Then why don't you get up?"

Archie came up less often than the others. Any kind of illness upset him, just as his mother's pregnancy upset him, and even disgusted him a little.

Dave wasn't old enough yet to have doubts. Despite his size, he was still a child. But it would happen to him, too, eventually. Would he let his son in on the secret? Would he have the courage to? Probably not. He suspected that everyone had to discover it for himself.

As for Florence, she seemed to be waiting, to be suspicious. Although she realized her father had somehow changed, she was reserving judgment until she knew more about it.

Was it because he had remained a poor small boy, innocent and uncomprehending, that she had despised him? He was sure now that she had despised him. He didn't blame her, either. He was too relieved that he had achieved a sort of peace with himself.

"Don't be in such a hurry to get up," said Nora one morning, seeing him standing by the bed. "You'll need all your energy next week."

"Why?"

"Miss Carroll ran after me as I was leaving the store. It seems they're expecting a visit next Monday or Tuesday: not just Mr. Larsen, but Mr. Schwartz, too. They're visiting all the branches."

"I'll be there."

"Of course. That's why you should rest till then."

Mr. Schwartz might well be a crook. He had no idea. But it was no concern of his. What difference could it make to him?

If Louisa had really been trying to give him a sign, she had failed. He would never again be hungry. He would never again smell the disgusting odor of the house on East 32nd Street. His wife and children would never know poverty.

And if he ever again was seized with disgust, or if things got out of control, why shouldn't he again deal with it by drinking, as most people did?

He himself would be shocked now if, for example, one of his staff . . . Of course! Couldn't it happen to Miss Carroll? She was sure to be disappointed by the new Higgins.

Well, there was nothing he could do about that. There was no turning back now.

And it was not beyond the bounds of possibility that one day, after keeping an eye on him for a while, *they*—Carney and the others—would come to ask him to join the country club.

"You seem better," remarked Nora.

"I feel better."

"I don't mean just physically."

"Neither do I."

Had she understood? He couldn't ask her. He wasn't yet sure that she *knew*.

"I can tell you now—you scared me."

"I scared myself."

"How do you mean?"

"It doesn't matter." He gave her a smile full of promise. "You'll see. From now on, everything's going to be all right," he said.

"I've never complained."

"I know."

"I trust you, Walter. I've always trusted you."

Did she mean she had always known that someday he would become a man like other men?

If so, she was going to be pleased with him, and so was Florence, and everyone in Williamson—and even Mr. Schwartz.

"You're the best man in the world."

That remained to be seen. He would have to pay the price, like everyone else.

But that was nobody's business but his own.

HINSDALE PUBLIC LIBRARY,
HINSDALE, ILLINOIS

Last activity date: 9/22/00
Total checkout:
Date: 8/17/04   20